WIMPS LIKE ME

By
TIMOTHY MARTIN

PublishAmerica
Baltimore

ISBN: 978-1-4489-7004-9
PUBLISHED BY PUBLISHAMERICA, LLLP
www.publishamerica.com
Baltimore

Printed in the United States of America

To Ernie, for being a father when I needed one most.
And to Wally and Raymond, my best friends.

Introduction

This was bound to happen sooner or later, one of those marriage, death, and taxes things. I don't know exactly where the urge came from. Fifty years of living in the Pacific Northwest might have something to do with it. Or maybe I banged my head harder than I thought last summer while repairing a broken water line under the house. All I know is that suddenly, more than anything else, I wanted to write a book about growing up in Humboldt County, California, a place where the air smells of rain, redwoods, and sawyers' cigars.

Humboldt County, which lies about 300 miles north of San Francisco, is one of the most scenic places on earth. It's also one of the most isolated. The roads leading into the area are narrow and crooked and the inhabitants few. There are hairpin turns and mountains jerking straight up out of the fields. There are pastures where horses graze and dairy cattle swing their tails, regarding you with large, liquid eyes. And all around, like a remote impenetrable fog, is wilderness. A green landscape that would give Tarzan pause.

Awe inspiring, yes, but when I was young boy there was a downside to all this beauty, a harsh reality that hangs in the memory like a fishhook. First there was the incessant rain. Morning and night we had misty, drizzly, depressing weather. It was the kind of weather that stayed around for months on end, until you were soaked and bored in equal parts. Until you eventually forgot that the sun ever existed.

Then there was the mill town I lived in. Scotia was a dumpy, cloud-hung, hind-end-of-nowhere town in one of the most economically challenged parts of the state. The streets were chuckholed, the driveways were gravel, and the drab little company homes were stacked cheek to jowl. There were dead cars on blocks and pickup trucks held together by prayer, primer paint, and rust.

The people who lived there were as sad as the town itself. They were wiry fishermen, poorly-educated sawyers, and grizzled loggers who stunk always of tobacco, sweat, and chainsaw oil. They were tired and overweight women who were constructed of hardship and despair. They were salt-of-the-earth folks, locked in a never-ending struggle to make ends meet. The citizens of Scotia led exhausting lives from dawn to dusk, ripping through trees with growling chainsaws, and drinking whiskey until they were nine times nine drunk. Some lost fingers to mill machinery. Others were crippled from lifting heavy lumber. Still others were killed in horrendous car accidents involving old-growth redwood trees that refused to budge. It was, in a word, pitiful.

Back then every town in Humboldt County had a sawmill, and every mill had a teepee burner rearing its head like a metal dinosaur into the damp and dreary sky. The mills were made up of ugly sawdust-covered corrugated tin buildings that were surrounded by a sea of lumber. There was lumber piled for sorting, lumber stacked for export, lumber hurtling toward planer knives—lumber everywhere, encircling our little town like the backdrop to a bad dream.

The sawmill in Scotia operated seven days a week, twenty four hours a day, ripping through logs and spewing out a constant billow of dust and smoke. I hated that mill. Everything about it bothered me. The smell of burning wood, the screaming saw blades, the overwhelming oppressiveness. There were times when I felt like taking a flame thrower and torching the whole place.

Depressing? You betcha. But the worst part was that I just didn't seem fit into the picture. People in Humboldt County were as tough as nickel steak. These folks didn't know the meaning of the word danger, much less how to spell it. I was a sensitive kid who watched TV, played with my chemistry set, and avoided pain and confrontation at all cost. Boys like me were a favorite target of school bullies, so I would make up stories about grizzly bear hunting with my imaginary father, or playing tackle football with my uncles, just to throw them off scent.

I guess you could call me a closet wimp.

There were a few others like me in town, quiet and unassuming boys who preferred comic books and a rousing game of chess over a freshly-killed deer or a bloody fistfight. We were milquetoast boys who did our best to survive in a world where cowards were despised and physical toughness reigned supreme.

The worst part? After high school graduation we were expected to stay in Scotia and work at the mill. Now, this may seem like a colorless little problem to most people, but for my money it was sanity stretched thin. How would you like to spend the rest of your days yanking ragged hunks of lumber off of a green chain? Clearly that wasn't the life for me. Better to jump off a high bridge. Or throw myself in front of a loaded logging truck.

Needless to say, I searched constantly for ways to free myself from that social Pleistocene tar pit of a town, away from the tree cutting, television praying, deer slaying, fish gaffing, reckless driving, loud shouting people who lived there.

Eventually I did get out. But then, oddly enough, I returned several years later. Why? Distance lends perspective, they say, and by then the unhappy and horrible had, in a strange way, mellowed into an amusing story. This is how it was that I arose one stormy morning, in the year before my 50th birthday, and embarked on a quest to revisit my childhood.

Which brings us to the book you hold in your hands, the story of a young boy hemmed in by a thick forest and ragged history; a bittersweet tale of bullies and best friends sprinkled with humor and sadness, happiness and anger; a full portrait of a child's life in a small Northern California logging town.

Hopefully, through the rich, vivid, Technicolor memories of youth, this book will allow you to taste childhood, to absorb it, and to appreciate the joys and sorrows of growing up in the Pacific Northwest.

Let's begin our journey.

Chapter One

I was five-years-old when my father disappeared. He left unexpectedly, vanished like a wisp of smoke, and I wasn't even sure who it was that stepped out of my life. I remember little about my dad. My mother refused to talk about him. She could scarcely bring herself to speak his name. It was as if he had simply disappeared from the face of the earth, or never existed.

That was the year my mother and I moved to Scotia. Unemployment there was endemic. Luckily, she found work at the mill. Her job was to stand beside the screaming knives of the board planer and feed rough planks into the machine. Each day she came home dirty, and so tired she had to rest in a chair before struggling to the shower. I didn't understand the complaints about the soreness in her arms. I didn't understand her frustration.

Sometimes my mother worked the night shift. On those evenings I whiled away most of my time in front of the television, watching programs like *The Brady Bunch* and *Father Knows Best*. There were no problems in those families. Everyone led happy lives. The children were good students and popular in school. They went to bed smiling and woke to a cheerful breakfast.

My own life was nothing like that. I hated school. My papers were marked not by good grades and stars, but with red circles and messages to "Put more effort into your work," and "Try harder." I kept to myself most of the time, never challenging anything or anyone. I believe that much of what was taken to be my soberness was simply a feeling of being on guard, of cautiously watching life flame around me. Of trying not to be too hurt or shocked at what might happen next.

What bothered me most was that I had no father. He had let us down. He had failed to do what a man was supposed to do. Work hard, pay his debts, and stand by his family. I grew secretive about my home life and never invited anyone over. I had an inexhaustible supply of excuses: There were chores to do and places I had to go. I had too much homework. Other times I created stories about my make-believe dad. He was strong, and he smoked cigars. He bought me a .22 rifle and we hunted rabbits together. He let me drink beer. Lies, big lies poured from my mouth like thick syrup.

My mother and I lived in an area just outside of Scotia where rent was cheap. Dry Gulch Road was a scruffy little warren of dingy, wood-frame homes located in a pull-yourselves-up-by-the-bootstraps neighborhood. Trash littered every yard, and soiled laundry hung from backyard clotheslines like the war-torn flags of third world nations.

Divorces, shouting matches, and drunken brawls were common events on Dry Gulch Road. Chaos swirled up and down the street like smoke off a battlefield. The entire place smelled of despair and heartbreak.

We lived at the far end of the road where it was mostly gravel and potholes. Logging trucks thundered past with regularity, mud flaps slapping, twin-stacks belching diesel smoke. Structurally speaking our house was much like those of our neighbors. The only difference was that my mother took pride in our little home, and in the yard that surrounded it.

Mom was a fanatic about a tidy yard, a compulsive fussbudget. Each morning she would take out her hoses and set them up with their little water sprinkling gizmos on the end. Whipping sprinklers whirred and sprayed, making rainbows that kept the grass green. After that, the lawn was fertilized and mowed short and close, until it looked sharp enough to inflict wounds. Meanwhile, I sat around twiddling my thumbs.

Dry Gulch Road was bor-*ing* especially during the summer months, when school was out. There were hardly any kids in the neighborhood. The Bagley twins lived a couple of houses down, but they were in kindergarten. Lester Pearbottom was just up the street, but his idea of a good time was beating the living crap out of you. Lester was big and mean, and, at the tender age of nine, already shaving. He specialized in knuckle-busters, nut-crackers, titty-twisters, and turning your face into a Grape Nehi fountain. I did my best to steer clear of him.

The only other kids on our street were our next-door-neighbors, the Spucklers. But they didn't count. Being seen in the company of a Spuckler was, on a scale of one to 10, a decimal point above coming down with a bad case of the flu.

Over the years an abyss had stretched between mom and the Spucklers. She called them a bunch of inbred, degenerate hillbillies with the morality of a pack of jackals. Mom had absolutely no patience for people who were lazy or apathetic.

She warned me about the Spucklers constantly, saying, "If I ever catch you in their yard, you'll be in big trouble, mister."

I wasn't deaf to her implied threats. I never went anywhere near the Spucklers house. But I did observe them from a distance. The patriarch of the family, Henry, was a long, bony man with a face that looked as if it had taken hundreds of invisible hooks and jabs in an anything goes brawl with time itself. Henry wore a full beard, pants tied up with a length of rope, and a big felt hat. His black eyes gleamed out of cavernous sockets, and a home rolled cigarette was forever cocked in the corner of his mouth. I'm pretty sure that Henry had never seen the inside of a schoolhouse. I don't think his wife, Mabel, had either.

Mabel Spuckler was a short, powerful woman. Her meaty arms swung like pendulums, and her feet were encased in big Gomer Pyle farmer shoes. She wore a dress that stretched and relaxed over a body that went far beyond the boundaries of ample. It was rumored that Mabel didn't believe in housework of any kind. This heresy deeply troubled my mother when she first heard it.

"That's why when they walk out of the house, you can see footprints on the porch," she said.

Mable was a user of smokeless tobacco. She kept a thick cut of Red Man working in her caving, toothless mouth at all times, and never came out of the house unless she had to spit. The woman was an expert at sending streams of russet juice great distances into the yard, often up to thirty feet. Whenever she rushed outside, tobacco bulging like a tumor in her jaw, she reminded me of a rhino trundling across an open stretch of African grassland.

Appearances aside, Mable was not an unfriendly person. She would always smile and wave at mom whenever she was in the yard. Her wave was met with a dour, disapproving scowl.

"I'm not about to make friends with the Spucklers," mom grumbled. "Not if all the seas dried up and the moon turned to zinc oxide."

Mable and Henry had a lot of children. How many? Who knows? A passel of them anyway. Barefoot, leaky eyed, runty kids always seemed to be coming and going; emaciated, sticky-looking youngsters with faces that only a mother could love, kneading mud into pies, dragging battered dolls through the yard, and leaping from the roof of their home.

Of the countless Spuckler children, I knew only two, Elmira and Cletus. Elmira was a child of stunning ugliness, an inherited mixture of bulging eyes and mashed-in nose, a frog-faced girl whose dresses were torn and shoes scuffed. It was plain that she had never been to the dentist. Her front teeth were buckled like a derailed train.

Elmira was a straight "D" student. She hated school, or anything that resembled work. Her favorite activity, I think, was expending as little energy as possible. She was very good at it. Elmira was lazy all right, but compared to her brother, Cletus, she looked like she was running around with flames shooting out of her rear end.

Cletus had skin as white as chicken dooky, dark, windowless eyes, and wore clothes that looked as if they had come off the damaged goods shelf of a disreputable second hand store. He spent the majority of his free time throwing rocks at his siblings or sitting cross-legged in the dirt with a lighter, burning the wings off of flies.

And dumb? Cletus was the only kid I knew who couldn't figure out a ball point pen. I guess I felt a little sorry for him. It was a shallow emotion, feeling sorry, but the best one I could summon up.

On top of their many shortcomings, the Spucklers were on welfare, and oh how mom hated that. She could think of nothing worse. Losing a loved one or having breast cancer didn't hold a candle to being on welfare. You could be dirt poor. You could spend your life scratching out a living. But at the bottom of everything, below even the septic tank, was a time when you might have to *go on welfare*. The Spucklers were, in fact, a second generation welfare family. To my mother this was proof positive that their genes and chromosomes were severely tainted.

All in all, the Spucklers were a pretty pitiful bunch. I don't think I ever heard anyone say a kind word on their behalf. I'm sure I never heard my mom say one. There was irony aplenty in the fact that they were our next-door neighbors. Their house was a monument to white trashery, a remarkably ugly two bedroom shanty that had no equivalent outside the third world. It was covered with rust brown asphalt shingles and had broken windows and blackberry vines creeping up the outside walls.

The yard was even worse. Over time it had been stomped to hard bare dirt, and where there wasn't dirt there were bald tires, bags of garbage, broken stoves, hollow televisions, rusting wrecks of cars and other imperishable effluvia that would no doubt be lying around several thousands years from now.

The Spucklers were the only family on Dry Gulch Road with an outhouse, one that put off a stink so concentrated it was nearly visible. The odor from that outhouse would have made a visit to local sewage treatment plant seem like a picnic downwind from the Old Spice factory.

"I'll sue them," mom threatened (and often choked) on hot summer days when things in the outhouse really got cooking. Of course, she never did. Mom never sued anyone in her life. She couldn't afford to, no more than she could afford to run for Congress. The Spucklers were trouble, but there was nothing she could do about it. They had settled like dirt in the nest of her knuckles and would not be easily washed away.

Everything the Spucklers did naturally turned out to be against the law. They never paid their bills. They never registered their automobiles. They never bought a dog license. And they stole things, sometimes right out from under our noses. First it was the hubcaps off of mom's '48 Rambler, both of them. After that it was a jerry can of gasoline, a tow chain, and a bumper jack, right out of our garage. Then it was a blackberry pie.

That's when things really began to heat up between the Spucklers and my mother.

It happened on a Sunday. I remember, because of all the days of the week I loathed Sunday the most. It's when Mom made me go to church. Pastor Brown's sermons were always on "Hell and Damnation" and "The Rapidly Approaching End." You could almost feel the fire and smell the brimstone as Pastor Brown clutched his bible and explained how unrepentant sinners would be inflicted with heart disease, cancer, and various ailments of the stomach and bowels. A question and answer period would follow, and I would ask myself, "What the heck am I doing here?"

The only good thing about Sunday was that mom would sometimes bake a blackberry pie before church and let it cool on the windowsill until we got home. That pie was almost worth the torture of enduring another of Pastor Brown's salvos on the miraculous healing power of the Lord, and the hellfire and hot coals that awaited sassy children, town drunkards, atheists and other non-believers.

On that particular Sunday we had just returned from church when mom let out a shout of alarm. Her blackberry pie was missing from the windowsill. She ran outside to investigate. When she returned her face was set in a peculiar way, expressionless but tight mouthed. It was the same grim face Grandma wore when she plucked the feathers off of a freshly-slaughtered Thanksgiving turkey. All clues pointed to the Spucklers. There was an empty pie tin in their yard and the whole clan was walking around wreathed in berry-stained smiles.

In short, the situation contained either a dead rat or one in rapidly failing health.

"Do you think the Spucklers took the pie?" I asked mom.

"Don't be an idiot," she said in typical endearing paternal fashion, "of course they took it."

The missing pie was only the beginning of our problems. Shortly afterwards, one of the Spuckler dogs snuck into our laundry room and whelped a litter of pups in a basket of clean clothes. When my mother saw the mess, she came unglued.

"Those people are the dog-gonest, low-downest, under-handedest excuse for human beings this side of Tony's Trailer Park," she cried. Mom was running on high octane hate at that point. Her face had turned a nice salmon color.

"Why don't you call the cops?" I suggested. She threw me a look that said dumb question.

"Call the cops? Our cops? Those guys couldn't pull a greasy string out of a cat's ear." Then she added, "Don't worry, I'll get even with the Spucklers. Just you wait and see."

Unfortunately, I don't think mom gave any real thought to the nature of the problem. These were backwoods folks she was dealing with, as down and dirty as you could get. She didn't know that when you pushed on people like the Spucklers, they would always roll back on you. Such was their specific gravity.

The first thing mom did was have a picket fence built on the boundary that separated our property. Then she hung "KEEP OUT." signs all over it. Not long after that several of the Spuckler kids started kicking the fence, working the pickets loose, cracking them like fire under an eager wind. Mom heard the commotion and came running. They high-tailed it home, laughing fiendishly.

My mother hated foul language, but she was as mad as Texas truck driver who'd heard a homosexual come back on his C.B. radio.

"Damn it," she said. "I'm not going to take much more of this."

As a rule lightning never strikes twice in the same place. But rules are made to be broken. Lightning sometimes will strike twice in the same place. And as if to prove that old saw about how often it does, a number of things began to happen to our fences.

In an attempt to dig the moat deeper, drive the stakes further down, push harder on the rock, mom had a sturdy chain link fence installed on our boundary line. Henry watched the fence go up, all the while dispensing a courteous smile. You could tell by the way he stood there that he had unlimited patience. He was the kind of man who could outlast floods and other natural disasters. Even his son, Cletus, had that maddening, gracious, old world patience.

It was an exhilarating experience, I can tell you, watching Henry drive right through that chain link fence a day later in his vomit-colored GMC pickup, plowing onto our lawn and smashing mom's prize dwarf apple tree in the process.

It happened just before midnight. I saw the whole thing from my bedroom window. Somehow mom slept through it. The next morning when she came out to turn on the sprinklers, her jaw must have dropped to her knees. She let out a scream that could be heard at the far end of Dry Gulch Road. I rushed outside. Henry Spuckler was still sitting in his pickup, passed out over the wheel. The smell of whiskey was heavy in the air.

"Is he drunk?" I asked, after mom had finally regained her calm.

"Of course he's drunk," she said. "When have you ever seen that man sober?"

Hours later, after Henry Spuckler finally woke up, he pulled the truck back into his own yard. It backfired and billowed exhaust from every orifice and portal. Mom picked up a rusted tailpipe and heaved it as far as she could onto the Spucklers property.

"Good riddance," she shouted.

Witnessing this scene, I turned to her and said, "Aren't you gonna call the cops?" The question earned me a cuff alongside the head that left my ears ringing like a bell tower.

The next morning mom did some serious thinking. "Ah-ha," she finally exclaimed. "There's more than one way to skin a cat." Then she picked up the phone and got busy. I wasn't sure what she had in mind, but the light above her head was plainly visible.

My mother's idea was to have another wall constructed. This one a row of cinder blocks. She threw herself into the task with an enthusiasm that bordered on delirium, helping the workers wherever she could in order to get the job done with greater speed.

After they were finished our little house looked more

secure than a medieval castle. The cinder block wall, however, was destroyed even before the concrete was dry. The Spucklers homed in on it like a heat-seeking missile.

Here's how it happened: Cletus was chasing his brother around the yard with his father's chainsaw when his attention was suddenly grabbed by the large redwood tree growing in their yard. The redwood had been there for years, over a hundred to be exact. It's just that Cletus had never really noticed it, at least not when he had a chainsaw in his mean little hands.

That's when he decided to play lumberjack and fall the tree-CRAAASH-right on top of mom's new cinder block wall. It was a noise that could be heard all the way over into the next county. When the smoke cleared there was a hole in the wall you could have maneuvered a bulldozer through.

This brought my mother bounding out the door. A slow, angry flush spread across her face. "Damn you people," she shouted, elocution not being one of her strong points at the moment. "Damn you all to hell!" Her eyes were spitting blue sparks that looked freshly dropped from an arc welder. Obscenities filled the air like small, godless black bugs. Then she stormed back inside and slammed the door so hard the report killed mice.

"I'm not done yet," she hissed. "Not by a long shot. If the Spucklers want a fight, then that's what they're going to get."

Chapter Two

Weeks went by before there were further problems. Then one morning the hell broth decided to erupt. Looking back—not just in a retrospective sense, but as you would at the rear end of a fully loaded logging truck that nearly ran over you—it was a miracle everyone came out of the adventure alive.

On the Big Day (which is how I came to think of it) dawn crept over the neighborhood cautiously, as if fearful of what it might uncover. The pungent smell of wood smoke from the Scotia sawmill filtered through on a gentle breeze. Robins twittered in the trees. Dogs barked fitfully, and cats sprawled on front porches, coughing up hair balls. Mom was on her hands and knees scrubbing the kitchen floor, an immortal posture, like the Marines raising the flag over Iwo Jima.

I was standing in the yard, wiping my bloody nose on the sleeve of my shirt. Lester had just chased me down Dry Gulch Road and beat me almost senseless. It was the third time that week. He was turning my face into a collection of assorted lumps.

As fate arranged it, that's when a little forked-horn buck strolled into our yard. It wasn't uncommon to see deer in our neighborhood. They came down from the hills to feed on apples in backyard orchards. But no deer in its right mind ever came within a mile of the Spucklers house, not unless it had a death wish. Evidently one wrong-minded animal did. It leaped our fence in a graceful bound and immediately set about cleaning up the windfalls under our damaged apple tree.

The Spucklers were milling around their house, much like they did the other six days of the week, when Henry happened to glance through the hole in our wall. He spotted the deer, a nice little three point buck, and the proverbial excrement immediately hit the proverbial fan.

Henry said, "Hot damn, a buck."

This brought Cletus around the house, and he shouted, "Where?"

Which brought Mabel to the kitchen window where she sent a powerful stream of tobacco juice into the yard and said, "Someone see a buck?"

Henry finally regained his senses and hollered, "Get the guns." Mabel fetched the shotgun from the bedroom, Cletus plucked the .22 rifle from behind the back door, and the two of them hustled outside.

Mabel was not nearly so spry and sure footed as she had once been. She stumbled over an old camshaft lying in the yard, but happily managed to catch herself on a sawhorse, and a little less happily managed to keep her hold on the shotgun, by the trigger.

BLAM! The eye-rattling blast of the .12 gauge was so unthinkably loud that it blew every other sound out of the air. The gun discharged in the general direction of our house so that Mabel almost bagged my mother, who had stepped out on the porch to see what was going on. The buck bolted, mom ducked, and our cat went flying across the yard, belly to the ground. A dinner plate sized hole appeared on the wall just behind mom's head.

The entire Spuckler clan was overcome in a fit of laughter. Evidently this was about the most hilarious thing they had ever seen. Henry laughed so hard he got caught in one of his phegmy coughs and spat into the weeds.

Funny stuff, yes indeed.

It was strange. Mom should have been cursing. She should have been shouting whatever wild insults came to mind. But she wasn't. The look on her face was one of gentle abstraction. It was the expression of a woman who was methodically unplugging herself from reality, one wire at a time. For long moments the only sound coming from our yard was the low, straw like *flip-flip-flip* of the lawn sprinklers. Then mom stepped inside. She had not uttered a solitary word.

"Aren't you at least gonna give 'em heck?" I asked from the door. But mom wasn't speaking. She had retired to the safety of her kitchen, and there she stayed for the remainder of the day.

That evening there was a tension in the house that was almost visible. I eased around my mother like a car moving past an accident on the highway. Later, she finally snapped out of it. Mom yanked herself from the kitchen chair, dashed outside, and let it fly. She shouted obscenities in the direction of the Spucklers house for a full thirty minutes, yelling so loud that the words were sacrificed to wholesale noise. Afterwards, like any boiler that had popped its safety valve, she felt better. I was just happy that everything was back to normal.

The next morning mom made me take an oath. I was never, ever, to talk, gesture, or communicate in any way with a Spuckler. Their name had officially become an unspeakable word under our roof.

A short time later, unbeknownst to mom, I broke that vow.

It happened on a Friday. I was outside, waiting to be called in for supper. The evening's repast was liver and onions. We ate certain things on the correct nights: Meatloaf with Elmer's Glue gravy on Mondays, Hamburger Helper on Tuesdays, Texas Six Gun Double-Toilet Chili on Wednesdays, Noodle-A-Roni on Thursdays, and liver and onions on Friday.

Liver and onions, for those who have never eaten it, is not one of those dishes that make a kid's mouth water with fretful anticipation. I always felt the cold creeps as Friday supper approached, knowing this dread delicacy would be put before me and I'd be told, "Just eat a little." Eating "a little" liver and onions, like vomiting "a little," was as bad as "a lot." My stomach lurched sideways at the mere thought of it.

Cletus was standing in his yard quietly picking his nose. The strains of country music leaked from an open window of his house. He peered through the hole in our wall.

"What ya doin'?" Cletus asked. His voice was nasal and hillbilly, a Jew's harp twanging in my ear.

"Nothin' much," I said. "And I ain't supposed to talk to you."

There was a long silence punctuated by the soft whooshing cadence of mom's lawn sprinklers jerking around and around. Cletus announced that he was double jointed. He proved it by pulling his thumb back until it touched his wrist.

"Unbelievable," I said. But of course I was thinking, big yawn.

"Wanna hear a dirty joke?" he said, moving closer.

"Nope," I replied.

"A pig fell in the mud. Get it?" He immediately repeated the joke ten times. I acted deaf, pretending complete absorption in my shoes. He smiled slightly without meeting my eye, motioning for me to come closer.

"Wanna go dig holes in the dirt?" he asked, still picking at his nose, which must have been some kind of a hobby with him.

"Nope," I said, trying to look preoccupied, if not totally oblivious. There was another moment of silence, during which time he struck pay dirt and flicked it off his finger.

"Wanna see my collection of cigarette butts?" he asked. Everyone in the Spuckler house over the age of six chain smoked cigarettes. Long term health effects were not a major concern in their family.

I pondered this for a while and then decided, "Naaaah." I wished he would go away. He gave his nose a short rest, reached into his pocket and came out with something.

"Want a Pixie Stick?"

Suddenly Cletus had my undivided attention. Mom never allowed me to have candy, but that didn't keep me from liking it. And I liked Pixie Sticks best. They were pure sugar in a straw. Colored, to make them nutritious, I think. They left your mouth pink and red and orange, like a baboon's butt. Pixie Sticks were to me what the voices of the Sirens had been to Ulysses.

"Heck, yes," I replied. He handed me a Pixie Stick. I bit the end off and sucked the sugar out.

"Your folks let you eat candy?" I said, amazed. Cletus smiled. The gaps between his teeth looked grouted.

"Shore do," he replied. "We even eat it fer supper."

"Candy? For supper?" Unbelievable. A miracle. I had heard nothing like it since Sunday school and the tale of the loaves and fishes.

"Come over later and I'll show ya," he said.

Come over? I knew that my chances of being able to fraternize with the Spucklers were less than zero. I could have gotten the tar wailed out of me for simply talking with Cletus. But what if it was true? What if they really did eat candy for supper? Why that would be worth a hundred, no, make that a thousand whippings just to witness such a sight.

"Okay," I said, "but I gotta ask my mom first."

"See ya' later," he replied, heading for his house. Of course, I had not the slightest intention of asking my mom if I could visit the Spucklers. No way. I simply went inside and told her that I was busy playing and didn't want supper."

"Alright," she said, "but the kitchen is officially

closed for the night." The rules in our house were that if you missed a meal there were no second chances. No coming back later to eat.

And thank God for that.

Checking over my shoulder several times to ensure I wasn't being watched, I crept through the hole in the wall and onto the Spucklers' property. An aura of mystery and danger hung over their house, Druidic, threatening. Just to be sure I was immune to all the germs about to be encountered I gave myself a cootie shot. Then I headed for the door.

Up close, the place was as ugly as something glimpsed through a rip in the canvas of a freak show tent. There was a dilapidated garage attached to one end of the house and a nest of bony, side-scuttling cur dogs chained to the porch. Penned wash, gray in the wind, hung on a tilting clothes line, and liberated chickens pecked the ground or sat inert, like swollen feather dusters. On top of all this (or should I say underfoot?), were junk cars, slick tires, soup cans, dead batteries, broken chairs, a hairless doll, bed springs, and dozens upon dozens of soiled diapers. Indescribable garbage was everywhere.

The dogs barked with hoarse and passionate intensity as I approached. A dirty cat ran out from under an expired clothes dryer, its tail up like an antenna. I worked my way around the dog turds in the yard, and past a Chevy Impala gutted by fire.

So far, so good, I thought, taking the stairs, two at a time, sawdust puffing from termite holes. The dogs strained on their leashes and vaulted about. I did a quick shave and haircut on the door.

No answer. I pushed the doorbell. It buzzed as if to scatter the countless rats housed in the lath and plaster behind the walls.

Still no answer. I was about to turn and run when Cletus came to the door, wiping his face with a sleeve. The dogs bounded about.

"Get down you mangy critters," he roared, kicking at them. "You lay down or I'll fill your hinder ends with bird shot so goldarn stiff you'll be crappin' B-Bs for a week." The dogs flinched and slunk away. Henry Spuckler was suddenly at the door. He leaned out, hawked back snot, twisted his head, and spat on the porch.

"Don't just stand there, boy," he said, "come on in."

I stepped inside the house and realized, at that moment, what it must have been like for Margaret Mead to stumble upon the Samoans. The Spuckler family was absolutely primitive. In addition to the naked, dirty-faced infant kids running about, the place was a helter-skelter mess of old furniture, rummage sale stuff, moldy walls, cats, cobwebs, and rolls of flypaper hanging from the ceiling like horror party decorations. The floor was covered with yellow linoleum, and broken windows were patched with cardboard.

In the kitchen there stood a grease-covered stove, a round shouldered refrigerator, and a sink crowded with pots, pans, and piles of other garbage. Numerous insects roamed at will.

But when I glanced at the Formica-topped dining room table, my whole impression of the Spucklers underwent a magical change. The table was piled high with pork 'n' beans, cocktail hot dogs, Milky Way bars, corn dogs, Neco

Wafers and a bowl full of Cheeze-Whiz, the lurid color of a school bus. A feast! And all this time I had thought the Spucklers had been living off of boiled bone soup.

"Gol dang," I croaked.

Mabel Spuckler was still bringing items from the kitchen: Twinkies in hot Log Cabin Syrup, potato chips, beer nuts, and Kool-Aid. With the appearance of each new course I oohed and aahed, as if watching a Fourth of July fireworks display. And it kept coming: Ding Dongs, Mountain Dew, pork rinds.

"Have you et' yet?" Mabel asked, shuffling over to the table, followed by a few of her favorite flies.

"No ma'am," I said, trying to sound as gee whiz as I could.

"Are you hongry?" I nodded with everything I had. I was as hungry as a wild dog. Cletus, calmly munching on a Hostess snowball, looked up and gestured for me to have a seat while he finished swallowing. I sat down next to him on a vinyl chair that had been knife-slashed and bandaged with electrical tape (a homey touch). Mabel handed me a plate and I loaded it with ice cream and powdered donuts. Two mouthfuls later I was in the most complete throes of ecstasy I had ever known. Delicious! I tore into the barbecue chips and washed them down with a bolt of Pepsi.

"Smelt like your ma was whippin' up liver 'n' onions fer supper," Henry said, complacently shoveling banana cream pie into his toothless maw.

"Yeah," I said, wincing at the remembrance as I licked away a strawberry milkshake mustache, "ain't it terrible?"

For the next hour, Mabel kept carting out the fine tasting victuals: Cheez Balls, fudge bars, French fries, orange soda, each item mixed amid my cries such as might have greeted a free trip to Disneyland or the crucified Messiah.

I thought of my mother. It would have made her very angry to see me at that moment, dining with the enemy. The very thought gave me gooseflesh. But angst or no angst, it wasn't hurting my appetite any. I was gorging myself on Dr. Pepper and Sweet Tarts as though I had just been shipwrecked for a month. I gobbled licorice whips like I had just been plucked from the edge of critical starvation.

So we ate. Deep dish pizza followed by a plate of macaroons, a bag of Chee-tos, and pound cake corralled around a mound of peanut butter cookies. It was at that moment that I found myself actually beginning to like the Spucklers.

We continued to eat: Yummy peanut brittle that would stick to my teeth for at least 25 days and actually fight decay while wrapped around my molars like wax Halloween teeth.

I felt closer and closer to this wonderful family with each mouthful, and did not stop whaling down food until I had eaten myself nearly sick. By the time I walked outside, past the dogs (who were extra friendly since I smelled like sugar), past the old bedsprings, broken bottles, discarded tin cans and general filth, I had a completely different impression of the Spucklers. They had taught me an important lesson: It's never good to judge people prematurely. You should always wait until you find out what they eat for dinner.

The next morning when I saw Cletus waiting for the school bus, I asked, "If supper is so good at your house, what do you eat for breakfast?"

"Breakfast is my favorite meal of the day," he replied through teeth partially glued shut with pink gum. "Just this mornin' we had Coke 'n' Oreo cream sandwiches 'n' Snickers bars 'n'—"

I guess I wasn't paying close attention, because I heard only a small part of the menu. My mind must was elsewhere, on more important matters. Such as how I could get Henry and Mabel Spuckler to adopt me.

Chapter Three

We moved back into town a few months later after my mother had saved some money, and an accident involving a choker-setter, a bottle of Old Crow whiskey and a falling redwood tree suddenly made company housing available. I didn't mind leaving Dry Gulch Road, not at all. The Spucklers had recently been evicted from their home for being late with rent, so the place held no further appeal for me. Besides, I was tired of being tormented by Lester. He had recently taken to tossing me into a patch of stinging nettles after beating the snot out of me. It was painful beyond words. I despised myself for being chicken and not fighting back, but I could never hope to trade blows with a bully the size of Lester. On a scale of meanness, he was off the chart.

That summer I met a kid named Wally Jones. Like me, Wally got picked on a lot. He had a weight problem and had been tagged with the cruel nickname of "Wobblin' Wally." We bumped into one another in the toy section of the Ben Franklin Five and Dime Store.

"Hey," I said. "My name's Cole."

"Hey," he replied. "I'm Wally." He studied me for a moment. "Aren't you the guy who got wedgied by Nate Johnson on the playground?"

I grimaced, painfully recalling just how far my underwear had traveled up into the crack of my butt that day.

"Yeah," I said. "Aren't you the guy who got dunked in the toilet by Skeeter Wilson?"

He frowned. "Yeah, Skeeter gave me a swirlie."

"That guy's a creep."

"He's a dork," agreed Wally.

Wally and I started hanging around together. We became best friends and co-wimps, well-versed in the art of slipping around bullies like Nate and Skeeter by using alleys, drainage ditches, and backyard fences to our best advantage. We also played Parcheesi and checkers, threw dirt clods at road signs, and raided our neighbor's fruit trees. But the thing we both enjoyed most was going to the movies.

A scary movie played at the Bijou Theater every Saturday night, and it was not to be missed. All week I would scrape together money by collecting pop bottles, selling whatever I could find, and digging out loose change from under the couch. Sometimes I came up short.

One weekend *The Killer Shrews* was playing and I really wanted to see it. The second feature was *Insects*, a movie about giant ants that no flamethrower could kill. It was the best double feature ever, and I needed two bucks (twenty-five cents for the movie, the rest for candy and soda pop). In an act of sheer desperation I went searching for work.

I spotted an unmowed lawn a few blocks from my house, strode up to the porch, and knocked. An old man answered.

"Yeah?" he said. He wore a stained John Deere cap. His jeans puckered beneath his tooled belt. The breast pocket of his T-shirt drooped with the weight of a package of Winston cigarettes.

"Want your lawn mowed?" I asked. He eyed me suspiciously.

"You playing hooky from school?"

"School's out," I said. "It's summer." He glanced up in the sky as though he hadn't noticed.

"Yeah, I guess it is."

I pointed a thumb back in the direction of his lawn. "Want me to mow your lawn?" I asked again.

"Where's your lawn mower?" he said. I didn't have a lawn mower, just a lot of youthful optimism.

"Ain't got one," I admitted.

"You know how to run a gas mower?"

"Yes, sir," I lied. I didn't want him to think I couldn't handle something that simple.

"I got a perfectly good one," he said. "Ain't used it in years. You can cut the lawn with that." He looked me over again. "You sure you want the job?" My fingers felt down in my pockets. Nothing but lint.

"Sure," I said. "How much?" His jaw took on a firm, thoughtful set.

"One dollar," he replied.

"This is a big yard," I said. "Look how high the grass is." He glanced out at the lawn.

"One-fifty, then."

"Two dollars," I countered.

His jaw dropped. "Two dollars? When I was your age

I worked from sunup to sundown and never made no two bucks."

I was not exactly a ball of fire in the brains department, arithmetic was a walk in the *Twilight Zone*, dividing fractions was a mystifying fall into the *Outer Limits*, but I knew how much a job like this was worth.

"I can't do it for less than two dollars," I said. His face drew up in a frustrated knot.

"All right," he grumbled, "two dollars. Follow me." He led me to the lawn mower, a primitive mechanical Yazoo nearly as old as its owner, with bike-sized rear wheels and a dangerously exposed blade.

I wheeled it out from the garage. The old man retreated to the porch to watch. First I filled the tank, spilling gasoline all over my hands. Then I yanked for a long time on the starter cord. Finally the machine stammered to life. It took one bite of the tough, fork tongued grass and died.

As I pulled and sweated as the old man stood to one side offering worthless advice. After some time I got it started again. I tilted the blade some and managed to cut out a mower-sized chunk of the weeds. Pulverized grass flew everywhere, coating me in fine green dust. I sneezed and wiped my nose on my shirt. The mower conked out.

The lawn was an endless jungle. It was a hot day, too. A lesser boy would've sizzled and popped open like a weenie on a grill in such heat. I didn't want to spend the whole day getting all sunburned and tired for a lousy two bucks, but I wanted to see that movie.

I sweated and struggled and finally started the mower again. The blade whined, biting into the snaky weeds, slinging gobs of grass through the air. I started chewing away at the edges of the jungle, carving a thicker slice with each pass around the perimeter. I raised a great grass cloud, and enough racket to drown out every cicada in town. Whenever I missed a spot, the old man would come down off his porch to point it out. Otherwise, I was all alone.

I mowed for an hour, or maybe it was two. My sense of time seemed to evaporate. The job swallowed me up and (here's the weird part) I actually started to enjoy it. I pushed back and forth across the yard, singing Elvis Presley songs in the key of the M (mower), stopping only to refill the gas tank. I was so caught up in the job, I almost forgot about the movie. But as soon as I had finished, I clutched the two dollars in my greedy little hand and sprinted for home.

When I told mom where I was going that evening, she frowned. "A monster movie?" she said. "Is that what's playing?"

"Aw, mom," I replied. I knew what was coming.

My mother hated scary moves. She was convinced that they contributed to nightmares and were a step-by-step recipe for juvenile delinquency.

"If only there wasn't so much violence," she said. "I wish Hollywood would show more happy movies."

"Geeze," I moaned, "who'd go to see something like that?"

Luckily, Mr. Fenwick, the theater owner, didn't share my mother's views. He never spoiled our Saturday nights with all-talk-and-no-action films. He showed movies like

Tarantula, Monster on the Campus, and *The Brain from Planet Arous* that were packed with thrills and terror, and had to be watched through spread fingers. Good old Mr. Fenwick.

Wally and I were the first ones in line that evening. We bought our tickets, rushed inside, and plunked ourselves down in the first row. There, in the close, expectant darkness of the theater, we shivered to the organist's opening chords and steeled ourselves for that first horrible look at a killer shrew (which turned out to resemble a hairless dog slathered in bacon grease).

The second feature, *Insects,* actually surpassed the first in over-the-top fear. It was a genetics-gone-crazy movie about huge ants that had been roused from their frozen sleep by an atomic bomb detonated at a research facility somewhere in Nevada.

Through it all, Wally and I sat spellbound. When "The End" finally appeared on the screen, we rose from our seats, stunned and shaken, to face the night.

"That wasn't so scary, was it?" I said, peering out into the darkness.

"Naw," Wally replied. "That blood was *so* fake."

"Yeah, and the guts, too."

"Especially the guts. They probably came from a dead pig or something."

There was a moment of silence. Then I asked, "Killer shrews can't really tear a human apart like that, can they?"

Wally took a quick glance over his shoulder to see if anything was following us. "I don't think so," he said, nervously.

And though both of us were trembling like aspen trees in a high wind, we walked home trying to convince ourselves that we hadn't been frightened by the movie. Not too much, anyway.

Wally and I did a lot of camping that summer. We considered ourselves master outdoorsmen, and often we would hike into an isolated area and survive with little more than a Swiss Army knife, a book of matches, and enough food to sustain the entire National Football League through a full week of practice.

Our camping trips were always a source of mystery to my mom. Part of the mystery was how a couple of kids who nearly died of exhaustion when asked to take out the trash, could lift such heavy packs. The other part was how we could eat so much food and still be hungry when we got home.

That morning we loaded our packs and set off up the trail like bumblebees in flight, honey bound. In the tradition of all hearty woodsmen, Wally and I allowed nothing but the weight of our packs to determine our final destination. When one of us would collapse, that place automatically became The Campsite.

As soon as we pitched camp, we would begin the sacred rituals of building a cooking pit, gathering firewood, and preparing dinner. Camp meals consisted of such delicacies as powdered soup in canteen water, ketchup (the only really good vegetable), beef jerky, and Spam coated with fire ash. All entrees were generously spiced with various low flying and curious insects. After dinner we sat beside the fire with our comic books and spent a pleasantly adventurous evening under the stars.

I took great pleasure in our camping trips. I didn't mind the smoke that blew in my face, regardless of wind direction. I wasn't bothered by the yellow jackets, mosquitoes, or ticks. And rainstorms had absolutely no effect on me. It was all great fun.

At least until it was time for bed.

As the first shadows of evening crept across camp, Wally laid out his bedroll. His sleeping bag was an authentic World War II souvenir from Beecham's Army-Navy Surplus Store. It was ripped entirely up one side (hand-to-hand combat?), riddled from one end to the other with holes (enemy machine-gun fire?), and it had a large red stain right in the center (soldier's blood?) But the most unbelievable thing about the bag—and we chuckled about this often—was that Wally had talked old man Beecham into selling it to him for the same price as an unused one. It was Wally's most prized possession.

My sleeping bag, however, was a big fat embarrassment. Actually, it wasn't even mine. It belonged to my six-year-old cousin, Sally. Since I didn't have my own bag, I was forced to mar the esthetics of our camping trips with hers. It was pink and white and covered from head to toe with pictures of those adorable bunnies, Flopsy, Mopsy, Cottontail, and Peter, standing in McGregor's vegetable garden. Not only was it as ugly as sin, it was nonfunctional, too. The stuffing consisted of either sawdust or horse hair, and when I climbed into it I simultaneously broke out in an itch and froze to death. I cannot describe my misery.

Wally had only one defect to his character. He had never learned the art of mincing words. When he saw my cousin's sleeping bag, he announced, "Looks like you're sleepin' with McGregor and his bunnies tonight, huh?"

"Very funny," I grumbled, climbing in and wiggling around to sort the lumps under me according to size and shape. As I grimly rode out the night, Wally snuggled deep into his authentic war bag and chuckled quietly to himself. More than anything I wanted a new sleeping bag. But not just any bag, mind you. I wanted the Bonanza Bag.

The Bonanza Bag had everything a kid could want. It was warm and roomy, and had a built-in pillow and a mosquito net head protector. Best of all, the bag was covered with full-color action shots of Ben, Adam, Little Joe, and Hoss, the whole Cartwright family from my favorite television show, *Bonanza!* Adam was leapfrogging over the rump of his horse. Little Joe was astride his mount with his hat low over his eyes. And Ben and Hoss were trading gunfire with a dozen sinister-looking villains.

Several times a week I rushed over to Tony's Sporting Goods to have a look at the Bonanza Bag. The shop was big, with a square window on each side and a double door between that opened with a clashing of bells. The windows were packed full of guns and fishing rods, basketballs and footballs, jackets and boots. I would bang through the door, bells rattling, and sprint to the rear of the store, past the duck decoys and boating supplies, to where the camping section was located.

There it was, in all its glory: the Bonanza Bag. Its outside lining was made of tough rip-proof nylon, and its inside was soft, sturdy cotton, and-

"Hey, kid, don't finger the sleepin' bags," shouted a voice from behind the counter.

It was the store owner, Mr. Sprull. He was tall, thin, and had a posture that resembled a jumbo shrimp. His hair was watered down so that it was plastered to his forehead. Mr. Sprull didn't like kids coming into his store. Especially kids with no money.

My eyes went back to the Bonanza Bag. I could see it all now. The campfire burned low, the stars overhead, sharp and silent, and me in my new sleeping bag, smiling, yawning, stretching luxuriously and popping my vertebrae. I was having an out-of-body experience when Mr. Sprull strolled over.

"Stand back a little, kid," he said, "you're startin' to drool."

A thought occurred to me. All the times I had been in the store ogling the Bonanza Bag, I had never thought to ask its price.

"How much is it?" I asked.

"More than you got in your piggybank, that's for sure."

Mr. Sprull had no more sense of humor than your average land turtle. He shifted a matchstick from one side of his mouth to the other. "Okay, if you gotta know, it's nineteen dollars and ninety-five cents."

Nineteen-ninety-five?" I cried. "Where will I ever get that kind of money?"

"You better find a job," Mr. Sprull replied.

I had mowed a lawn before, so the concept of work was not entirely new to me. But I had done that only out of sheer necessity (no money, no movie). The sad truth of it was that I hated work. And I vowed to never exert myself again, for the remainder of my life. Still, if I wanted a Bonanza Bag, I had to raise some cash fast. I decided to break my vow and find a job.

Horace Skinflint was a local rancher with black eyebrows and a rumbling voice who often hired kids to help with chores. I broke down and indentured myself to him at the rate of twenty-five cents an hour changing irrigation pipe and mending fences.

It took forever to earn $19.95. And at the end of the very hour in which I earned the last quarter that I needed, I immediately resigned my position and told Horace that I would never be back.

With cash in hand, I sprinted back to the store and slapped it on the counter.

"There," I said, "hand over my Bonanza Bag, please."

Mr. Sprull slowly counted the money. "Ya' ain't got enough, kid."

"What?" My jaw dropped. "It's $19.95. That's what you said a Bonanza Bag cost."

"Ya' forgot the tax."

"Tax?" I said.

"Yeah," he said, "for the gov'ment."

And so it was that I learned my first hard lesson about Uncle Sam and giving until it hurts. I also learned what it's like to crawl back to a heartless man like Horace Skinflint. Would he put me back to work? Sure he would. You bet.

Only this time I would be shoveling cow manure for ten cents an hour.

Somehow I stuck with the job, earned the rest of the money, and bought the Bonanza Bag shortly thereafter. Of course I never told Wally. Then, on our final camping trip that summer, just before bed, I unrolled my Bonanza Bag with a flourish and stood back. His eyes fastened on it like a matched set of vises.

"Whoa," he said. "Where did you get that?"

"Aw, it's just a little something I picked up at Tony's," I replied.

Wally whistled through his teeth. "Man, she's a beauty."

It was plain to see I had earned my companion's everlasting respect. And when I climbed into my sleeping bag for the first time, Oh, the ecstasy! The pure, sensual delight! It was like slipping into the arms of an angel.

As good fortune would have it, the mosquitoes were thicker than usual that evening. Safe inside my Bonanza Bag with the patent mosquito netting covering my head and the Cartwright clan standing guard over my body, nothing could touch me. Wally, on the other hand, spent most of the night slapping at insects and cursing silently to himself.

Just before I drifted off to sleep, I could have sworn that I saw a single tear trickle down Wally's cheek. It was hard to tell, though, because of the dark cloud of mosquitoes circling his head.

Chapter Four

When Wally moved away I was heartbroken. His father, a sawyer for Pacific Lumber Company, had found a better-paying job at a mill in Myers Flat. They hooked a trailer to their family sedan, loaded it with their meager possessions, and pulled out of town. I waved good-bye to Wally as they drove off. That was the last I would ever see of him.

It was lonely without my friend, and a lot more dangerous, too. With no one to watch my back, bullies like Nate and Skeeter honed in on me like heat-seeking missiles. In order to escape their merciless beatings I found myself spending more and more time hiding out. And the best place to do that, I discovered, was the Eel River.

The river was less than a mile from our house. It dipped out of the mountains to the east and slid past our small town. The Eel pooled in long, shadowed clefts beneath the shoulders of hills and dug its own small canyons. The river was anything but boring. It was a place I could gambol away entire afternoons capturing frogs and skipping rocks. I could stretch an hour to three hours by swimming and exploring. Seldom did a summer day pass that didn't find me trudging through the woods, smashing my shins against fallen tree trunks and collecting temporary Heidelberg dueling scars from the brambles that crowded the path, headed for the river.

On those days I was often up before my mother. From my window I could see the sun rising, the ground mist filling with light. The silver notes of a quail drifted in from the garden. I dressed with lightning speed and rushed for the door, pausing only long enough to toss a few sandwiches into a paper bag.

To get to the river I had to cut through Ole Thornton's cow pasture. It may not have been the easiest way to the river, but it kept me out of sight. Instead of going by way of roads and trails, I took short cuts, bippity-bopping along through pastures and over fences. I kind of liked getting there the hard way, the adventurous way. And sneaking through Ole's pasture was always an adventure.

Ole was a grumpy old farmer and every fence on his property was posted, reading from top to bottom, "No Hunting," "No Fishing," and finally, as an afterthought, "No Trespassing." I dove under the barbed wire fence and wove happily across the field, grasshoppers bursting up from under my feet and whirring off, cracking like the playing cards I put on my bicycle wheel spokes.

The pasture eventually gave way to woods. I ran in and out of the sunlight, under the shadows of trees, where the forest floor was soft with richness and held a whispering of the smells of a hundred years of decay. A bird darted through the underbrush ahead of me. A cottontail rabbit bounded into view, froze, and leaped away. My destination was just ahead.

I could always smell the river long before I could see it. The air swelled with the sweet, damp scent of water as heat gave way to green coolness. I ran the remainder of the way, twigs clutching at my trousers, berry vines ripping at my shins, low branches whipping my face in tiny star bursts of pain. Then I bulled my way through a final patch of dense underbrush and stood at the river's edge.

My favorite spot on the Eel River was a sandy beach just upstream from a good fishing hole. It was popping with life there. Midges swarmed over the water and caddis fly larvae in their cylinder homes crawled along the bottom. Sedges and bulrushes grew along the bank, cooled by the lazy current, and water striders silently patrolled the surface. In the branches above, noisy birds gargled bug juice.

Small wonder that I came to this spot again and again, as to an oracle. There were so many fun things to do. I leaned against a big rock and watched a kingfisher fly over, searching for a meal. I watched a dandelion puffball blow across the water, fall to the surface and rise again, too light to break the surface tension. Then I took out my yo-yo, did a few around the worlds, and let it sleep for a while. After that I caught a lizard and held it in my palms. Its dry head bumped frantically against my fingers.

By noon the crickets were buzzing in the grass and I could feel the burning sun on my eyelids. Sweat trickled off my forehead. It was time to cool down. I peeled off my clothes and dove in. I never brought a swimsuit to the river with me. That was part of the fun. Skinny-dipping was a freedom that most people today would trade their right arm for.

Of course, there was one small danger involved. The river was thought to be inhabited by large snapping turtles, who with their bony overbite could snap off a kid's toe. Or worse! And though in all my days on the river I had never seen a turtle, snapping or otherwise, I had no doubt of their existence.

Was I worried about being bit by one of those little horny-beaked reptiles? Heck, yes. But the river held special powers. "I'm cool, I'm refreshing, I'm inviting," the water murmured, as pole willows arched long graceful limbs out over its surface.

Snapping turtles? If the Loch Ness Monster itself had been frolicking in those waters it would have had to share them with me. I dove in, leaving far behind on the surface the dancing shadows of the trees. I didn't see any snapping turtles that day, but I did share the river with a family of otters and a great blue heron. I swam for long, refreshing hours. By the time I dried off, the sun was plunging into the canopy of trees to the west and the day was melting into buttery evening.

Finally, hating to go, wanting to wring the last drop from the day, I sat on the bank and watched a tangerine peel of dusk swirl down the drain behind the mountains. Then I pulled on my clothes and started for home. My shoes were colored the green of forests, and my hands were coated with the good smell of grass and earth.

I only wished Wally could have been there to enjoy those days with me.

Summer soon ended and it was back to the drudgery of school, and dodging bullies. One afternoon a kid named Rudy Griddle cornered me in cafeteria and noogied my head until it was raw. Then Sash Ravens wailed the tar out of me in the boy's bathroom. Each day was a new worry, with little to look forward to besides another beating at the hands of some grade school Neanderthal. I walked around ready to flinch from blows that could come at any moment, and from any direction. Those were tough times for a kid like me.

Actually, times were tough for everyone in Scotia. There had been layoffs at the mill and the gypo logging outfits had stopped cutting timber. Everyone was strapped for cash. On top of the layoffs, the rain was eager that year. Two weeks before Thanksgiving a storm blew in, flooding the rivers and ruining the fishing. It had all the earmarks of being a long, hard winter.

People say that love makes the world go around, but they're wrong. Hope is what made our world go around. In Scotia our hopes were basic. We hoped that the mill would start hiring again and that the rivers would clear so we could fish. Hunting was a kind of hope, too. When people hunted, they hoped there would be a deer for the freezer. Sometimes it seemed like there never was, especially when the warden came nosing around.

Deer season was when the game warden started combing the hills in his dark green pickup. The cooler months were when the whitetail deer began putting on weight, when their size grew and their coats became thicker. It was also when my Uncle Howard hunted to make it through the lean months. Sometimes he would drop by the house and bring us venison. Whenever he did, I would beg him to take me hunting. At first he refused, probably thinking I was too weak to even hold a gun. Eventually, though (and with no small amount of prodding on my part), he gave in.

In order to clear the hunting trip with my mother, Uncle Howard made up a lie. He told her we were going to do some target practice.

"You know how I feel about guns," my mother said. "They're dangerous."

"We'll be at the shooting range," he replied. "It'll be perfectly safe."

Uncle Howard had a good reason to lie. He was a road hunter who took his deer out of season, without a license. He searched for them on the logging roads, and dropped them with a .22 rifle. My mother had no idea that her brother hunted illegally. If she had known, I would have never been allowed to go with him.

The man whose job it was to catch poachers was the local game warden, Gene Phelps. When he wasn't too drunk to find his badge, or too hung over to keep his pickup out of the ditch, Phelps patrolled the back roads of Humboldt County searching for hunters like my uncle.

No one knew much about Warden Phelps. He had wide shoulders and a square face, like a detective in a comic strip, and he took his job seriously. We knew that much. When Phelps caught someone poaching, he didn't cut them slack. It was automatic jail time and a $500 fine. It didn't matter if a guy was disabled or out of work. It didn't matter that he had five kids to feed or a wife dying of cancer. Nothing mattered to Warden Phelps except catching poachers.

The law didn't keep people like my uncle from hunting, not when beef was going for up to eighty five cents a pound. Not when venison was about the only thing families could afford. Most of the people in town had never owned a hunting license. They were barely scratching out a living. Why pay for meat when you could get it for free?

Uncle Howard didn't like poaching deer. Before his injury, he had been one of the best timber fallers in Scotia. His arms were layered with muscles and his hands were a terrain of calluses and scars. He had worked in the woods for 20 years before ruining his back by toting a seventy pound chain saw over a slash pile. He never got disability benefits or unemployment. What he got was a severance check and a boot in the butt from a company that had no use for crippled employees.

My uncle may have been stove-up, but I was told that he could take care of himself in a fight. One night he went up against three construction workers in the parking lot outside of Slim's Bar.

I never heard how the fight started that night, but I was told that the construction workers came at Uncle Howard with fists and bottles. He made short work of those men, dropping each of them like a sack of rocks, bam-bam-bam—just like that. It was over in seconds. Then he helped them to their feet and bought a round of beer. That's the kind of man my uncle was, a good man. Not like Tommy Krebs.

Tommy was Uncle Howard's hunting partner. He had long, scraggly hair, hard cheekbones, and dark brown eyes, like mud at the bottom of a slow running stream. According to my uncle, Tommy was a real screw up. He got hooked on the bottle about the time he dropped out of high school. On his sixteenth birthday he went on a bender and lost his driver's license. He almost lost his life. Tommy was on his way home from a tonk bar when he fell asleep at the wheel and wrapped his pickup around a tree. He was laid up in the hospital for almost a year. After that, he spent another six months in alcohol rehab. He went right back to drinking as soon as he hit the street.

Tommy was one of those people who liked to prove himself by picking fights. He would blind-side punch a man and kick him in the ribs as he fell, just to keep him down. Tommy was mean crazy, all right, but when he was on the business end of a rifle there was no better shot. When he hit a deer it went down for good. That's why Uncle Howard took him hunting with us.

Chapter Five

We left town at 7 A.M., moving past old wood frame houses, mobile homes, and gaping vacant lots piled with decaying lumber. Then Scotia disappeared and the road stretched out before us, empty and gray. We were in Uncle Howard's pickup, a battered and dented Ford F-100 with mud tires and no plates. The truck wasn't much to look at, but it would take you anywhere you wanted to go and back out again.

My uncle was driving. I rode shotgun. Beside me, Tommy groaned, stiffened his arms and pushed back against the seat. He was nursing a bad hangover. He had been drinking the night before, knocking back high tension booze until the wee hours of the morning. The smell coming off him was almost flammable. Uncle Howard had to pull off the road every few miles so that Tony could climb out and throw up in the weeds.

From the main highway, the truck veered left onto Burnchurch Lane. A mile or so later we turned onto an abandoned logging road that was wildly overgrown and full of deep ruts. Navigating it, the pickup wallowed and pitched like a ship in choppy seas. Uncle Howard low geared up the inclines so as not to high center on the rocks. I watched the clearings and draws for signs of deer. It didn't take long to find them.

We rounded a turn and I spotted two does next to the tree line. In the morning light they were almost invisible, their gray coats blending perfectly against the tall grass.

I shouted "Deer," and Tommy came alive. He grabbed the rifle, hopped out of the truck, and plugged them both, dead as hammers right through the heart. Quickly, we slit their throats and threw them in the back of the truck. Then we got out of there.

The job went as smooth as silk. The only thing left to do was field dress the animals. Uncle Howard drove down the road a short ways and pulled off into the brush where no one could see us. That's when it started to rain.

The clouds, which had been hanging over us since morning, broke with a roar of thunder. Rain cascaded against the truck windows in splashes like fistfuls of water thrown by an invisible hand. No one had been smart enough to bring a rain jacket so we decided to wait out the storm. Uncle Howard clicked on the radio. Tommy pulled out a pint of booze, uncapped it, and took a couple of quick swallows. The spicy hot smell of the whiskey filled the cab. Tommy held out the bottle.

"Have a snort, Howard," he said. My uncle regarded the bottle.

"I guess there ain't nothin' better to do," he grumbled. "At least until the rain lets up."

The bottle went back and forth between them a few times as the storm thickened and covered the truck in a rush of water. Tommy lit a cigarette and let the smoke feather through his nose and drift out the wing window.

"I hope this weather clears soon," said Uncle Howard, peering through the rain-streaked windshield. "I'd like to get them deer cleaned and get out a here."

"Take it easy," Tommy replied. "We got plenty of time."

Uncle Howard frowned. "You got time. I got things to do."

"That's the trouble with you," said Tommy. "Everything's work. You gotta learn to cut loose and have some fun once in awhile."

They sat there awhile, taking pulls off of the bottle. Outside, the rain chewed gullies in the ground, turning the hard clay into a dirty yellow paste. The top of the windshield was breath fogged. The radio was playing a song by The Drifters, *Up On A Roof.*

"Listen to this, will you?" Tommy said, reaching for the volume knob. "Here's my favorite part." The Drifters were singing *When I come home feelin' tired and beat, I go up where the air is fresh and sweet-*

Tommy leaned his head back and closed his eyes. "You oughta pay attention," he said. "There's a lot of wisdom in that song."

The rain wasn't letting up. It needled down at an angry slant. Shifting wind drilled water against the truck. Uncle Howard grew restless. He pulled his cap tight onto his head and grabbed a knife.

"Come on," he said, "those deer ain't gonna' skin themselves."

"Hold up," said Tommy, "I ain't gettin' out in that

weather until I'm properly lubricated." He uncapped the whiskey and took a long pull. When he was done only an inch of liquor sloshed in the bottle.

Uncle Howard opened the door and said, "Okay, let's hit it." We pulled ourselves out into the cold. Mud sucked at our boots. Rain pelted against our backs. I clamped my teeth and tried not to shiver. My uncle grabbed one doe by the fetlocks and yanked it out of the truck bed. I grabbed the other and strained against the weight. Tommy threw a length of rope over a tree limb and we strung one doe up by its hind legs.

We were hoisting up the second deer when Uncle Howard stiffened. He leaned forward, head cocked. "Listen," he said.

From far off came the grumble of a motor working hard in low gear. Tommy grabbed the rifle from the truck cab. My uncle snatched up the binoculars. The three of us moved uphill for a better view, climbing toward a knoll that poked out above the surrounding trees.

At the crest of the knoll Tommy and I found shelter beneath the branches of a fir tree. Uncle Howard watched through his binoculars. I could see the breath puffing from his lips, rising over the curve of his nose. Beads of water had collected on his lashes.

"It's the warden," he said.

I crawled over to Uncle Howard and he handed me the binoculars. On the road below sat a green pickup with a star painted on its side. The warden climbed out. He wore a badge on the outside of his rain jacket and a Smoky Bear hat. He was holding a rifle. Walking away from the bluff with his back to us, the warden surveyed the landscape. Then he turned, staggering slightly.

Tommy unfolded from his squat and came over. He took the binoculars and studied the warden.

"He won't be no problem," said Tommy. "That old boy is shit-faced. He's as drunk as Cooter Brown."

Uncle Howard and I grinned, and Tommy repeated himself, drawing another round of head shakes and chuckles.

The warden circled through the rain stripped trees, hesitated, and climbed back in his truck. He drove off with the red taillights of his pickup dwindling in the heavy rain.

I was shaking hard, and not just from the cold. "He's leaving," I said. "Do you think he saw us?"

"Nah," said Tommy, pulling the bottle out of his pocket and awarding himself another portion of whiskey. "He didn't see diddly-squat."

"Don't underestimate that old boy," said Uncle Howard, squinting through the rain. "I've heard he's smart as a snake."

"Hell," said Tommy, "the only thing we got to worry about is getting them deer skinned." We stood there for a moment, leaning against the icy water that rushed down at us.

Finally my uncle stood up, knee joints popping. "All right," he said, "let's get busy."

Our plan seemed foolproof. Uncle Howard and I would skin the deer while Tommy stood guard on the hill, making sure the warden didn't double back. If he did come around, Tommy would whistle to warn us and we'd head for cover. We eased down the bluff and got right to work, tussling the second deer up into the branches of the tree. Then I held the ropes steady as Uncle Howard pulled out his knife and began field dressing the animals.

The weather refused to let up. It was a hard perpetual rain, a streaming downpour. My uncle worked quickly, licking at the drops of water that slid down his cheeks and tickled the corners of his mouth, straightening up now and then to stretch the kinks out of his back and curse the cold.

Neither of us was thinking about the warden. We had no idea he was anywhere about until he spoke. I think what he said was, "I'll be a son of a gun."

At first I felt panic. The raw, fluttery panic of a bird trapped in a garage. Uncle Howard must have felt it too. For a few seconds nobody said anything. I stood there, trying to wipe the water from my eyes.

"Well, now, by ding." the warden drawled. "I knew I'd catch you boys sooner or later. I knew I'd get you."

"What are you gonna do with us?" asked Uncle Howard.

Rain trickled down the warden's cheeks. He was cautious and watchful, like a rattlesnake when he's about to let you have it. "I'm fixing to run you in for poaching," he replied.

"You could just let us go," said my uncle. "We only take what we need to eat."

The warden glanced over at the half-skinned deer hanging in the trees. "I bet you'd like that, wouldn't you?" he said in mock sympathy. "You'd like it if I'd just let you boys mosey on out of here. Well, that ain't gonna happen. You're goin' to jail."

He seemed to be enjoying himself. That was obvious from the look on his face. I was as scared as I've ever been in my life, and shivering harder than ever. I knew that day how a treed cougar feels, snarling and spitting at the hounds. And the hunter standing there, watching, and taking his sweet time. That's when you want to yell and run, do something stupid, just to end the tightness. But I wasn't going to do anything like that, not with a rifle pointed at me.

He stared at us and said, "This ain't no schoolboy prank, you know." Then he moved his gun so that he held it at waist level. "You two are breaking the law here."

"It's not exactly," Uncle Howard told him. "We just shoot this venison because we can't afford to buy meat."

"Don't smart mouth me, boy," he said. "What I want you to do is clean that blood off your hands and follow me." He raised the rifle in his hand, the first time he'd made a move that seemed menacing. "You're under arrest for hunting without a license and shooting deer out of season."

My uncle started for a puddle of water. The warden brought his gun up. "And don't think of making a run for it."

Uncle Howard eyes were dark. He chewed on his bottom lip for a second. "Warden," he said, "I reckon I'm in enough hot water already. I ain't about to go looking for anymore."

I stood there, frightened out of my wits, trying to think of something to say that would make him turn us loose, to let him know that what we were doing was better than stealing or being on welfare.

I was thinking hard when he asked me, "What the hell does a young boy like you get from breaking the law?"

"He was just along for the ride," said Uncle Howard. "I reckon I shouldn't have brought him."

The warden smiled again and spit tobacco juice. He wiped his mouth with the back of his sleeve and brushed his hand against the side of his pants.

"Ain't that the truth," he chuckled.

The warden opened his mouth to speak again but was cut short by the sharp crack of a .22 rifle. I remember thinking that it sounded like a branch snapping. Then another shot came, kicking up water in front of the warden's feet.

"Huh?" he grunted, whirling around. "What the—" He saw Tommy out toward the edge of the trees. We all saw him, running, crouched low. And then he disappeared behind a pile of brush.

"What's that fool shooting for?" the warden said. Another bullet hit close to his feet and he jumped.

"Damn you," he shouted, raising his rifle. He shot into the brush Tommy had jumped behind. The rolling boom of his deer rifle sounded loud after the short crack of Tommy's .22.

He threw us a cold look but kept his gun pointed at the brush. "If that boy's a friend of yours, you better tell him to lay down that weapon."

An angry spear of lightning split the sky like a flashbulb on a giant's camera. Then Tommy was running again, sprinting toward a stand of trees. The warden shot at him again, though he didn't seem to take aim. Tommy disappeared into the brush. My uncle reached out to grab his rifle but the warden saw him coming and yanked it away.

"Stand back," he said. His gun was raised to slam Uncle Howard on the side of the head. He threw his hands up to protect himself. The warden laughed with a grunting sound and the gun barrel whipped into my uncle's stomach. He went down on his knees, doubled over. From out in the brush we heard Tommy yelling at the warden.

"Phelps. Hey, you old drunk. Let them go or I'll drill a bullet straight up your ass." I watched the warden's face twist from one angry expression into another one. He took a step toward Tommy's voice.

"Damn white trash," he shouted back. "I'll teach you a thing or two when I get you down here." When Tommy yelled again, the warden fired several shots into the trees. I stood there, shivering violently, knowing we'd find Tommy lying on the ground with a big bullet hole in him. Uncle Howard hollered for him to give it up and come in.

"Run," Tommy shouted back. "I'll take care of him."

I thought about it for a second, but after hearing the sound of the warden's gun I wasn't about to move. Uncle Howard didn't seem to have any such ideas either. He stood there, staring out toward the edge of the trees.

The warden was down on one knee now, shoving more shells into his rifle. Rain poured down his face. He said to us, "You'd better call that boy in. Otherwise, I'm going to kill 'em." Then he tightened his eyes into hard little twigs, looked off toward the trees, and yelled, "Throw down that rifle and come out. You hear me?"

It was quiet for a minute. Then Tommy laughed. "Screw you," he shouted back.

The warden's lungs expanded his barrel chest to its fullest capacity, and he exhaled loudly with gale force, like someone preparing to swim a long way under water.

"This is your last chance, boy," he said. "Toss down that gun before you get hurt."

Tommy didn't have enough imagination to be scared, I thought. Or enough experience. Young guys like him just can't believe that they're ever going to die. Everyone else is, but not them. They think they can survive anything that's thrown at them, including bullets.

The warden stood there for a long moment, muttering curses. Then he began to pull the trigger as fast as he could. He fired six, seven times. I don't know how many bullets he shot. All I could hear was the noise of that gun going off, and its echo booming against the surrounding mountains. Suddenly he lowered his rifle and turned to look at Uncle Howard and me. His jaw dropped open and his eyes were wide.

"Oh Christ," he said, falling to his knees. I hadn't been able to hear Tommy shooting over the boom of the rifle, but now I could see he had been. The warden pulled himself to his feet and leaned against a tree, his gun hanging at his side. There was an ugly heaving to his chest, a losing struggle for breath. The shuddering of it was something to make you sick. He closed his eyes and breathed in deep a couple of times. I wanted to do two things at once. One was to turn and run. The other was to see if I could help him. I stepped toward him, but he moved his legs around and fiddled with his gun in a way I didn't like, so I stopped. The warden edged around to one side, still leaning his shoulder against the trunk of the tree, and looked right at us.

"I oughta shoot you boys," he whispered. "I oughta kill you right now." He coughed up bright red blood. Then he closed his eyes again and the tip of his rifle sunk to his foot. His eyes opened slowly, and I could tell he was still seeing us, but I thought for sure he was dying. I felt my legs shaking. What I was seeing suddenly went black around the edges and I was afraid I'd fall.

Uncle Howard came to my shoulder. He said something but I couldn't hear. It was like nothing inside me was working. All I could see was the warden slumped against that tree with his eyes shut tight, his teeth clenched, and rain running down his face. Then he fell to the ground, face first.

My uncle stepped forward. He reached down and turned the warden over. His chest spurted a red arc. Then another. The blood trickled into a puddle, turning the water pink. Uncle Howard went back out to the clearing, his back to me, hands cupped around his mouth so his voice would carry.

"Tommy, come on in. This guy's dying."

Seconds later Tommy came running in. "What happened?" he said. "Did I hit him?" We stood there for a moment, staring at the warden. Dark rain trickled from his eye sockets. Blood soaked the earth. Uncle Howard bent down to check his pulse.

"Nothing," he said. "He's gone."

I sat down on a log. My eyes were watering so bad I was almost blind. I got them cleared, finally, and started thinking again, my mind moving in circles as it tried to latch onto something hopeful. Tommy shook his head. His eyes were glazed with worry.

"I didn't mean to kill him," he said. "Honest to God, I was just trying to scare him off." Rain continued to drop straight from the sky as if following ropes to earth. My uncle blew water from his lips.

"You did a whole lot more than scare him off," he said.

"I can't believe I hit him," Tommy said. "I wasn't even aiming."

For a moment it was quiet. Then Uncle Howard spoke. "I say we just leave him be."

"What if someone finds him?" Tommy asked.

"They can't prove it was us."

Tommy shook his head. "There's quite a few folks around that know what we do," he said.

"That's nothing to say somebody else couldn't have done it this time," replied Uncle Howard.

"God, I'm just as sorry as hell," Tommy said. "You believe me, don't you? You know I was only trying to scare him."

"I believe you," Uncle Howard said, "but I don't think anyone else will."

I stared at the warden, lying on his back next to the tree. I stood there for a long time, listening to the rain and thinking with that extra clarity fear gives you.

Tommy nodded. "You're right. No one will believe us."

"Okay," said Uncle Howard, "let's get out of here."

We tossed our gear in the pickup and climbed in the cab.

"Do you think they'll track us?" Tommy asked. His mouth moved slow, like he had a toothache.

"Not if we're careful," my uncle said. "And not if this rainstorm keeps up."

Uncle Howard started the engine. I was suddenly cold. I held my wet shirt away from my body and thought about what had happened. Curls of steam rose from the warming hood. A steady hum of rain beat against the truck. Uncle Howard looked over at us.

"We're in this together," he said. "The one thing we've got to keep remembering is that."

We made a vow then and there, a promise to deny everything, even if we weren't believed. I knew Uncle Howard was worried about me, thinking I would be the one to break the vow and run to the police. But I kept quiet. I never told anyone what happened that day, not even my mother. Keeping that promise would be my first sad step toward manhood.

I soon learned there would be many more to follow.

Chapter Six

When I turned thirteen, I ran with a kid named Raymond
Sproat. We became friends, classmates in the eighth grade.
Raymond was willowy and dark-skinned, and had eyes the
color of cinnamon toast. He was the coolest kid I had ever
known. He used foul language, smoked cigarettes, and stole
money from his parents. He would do the wildest things,
take the craziest chances. Raymond cheated on exams, cut
classes, and picked fights with kids twice his size. He had
a scar on his chin from where he dove from a bridge and
hit the bottom of the river.

We hung around a lot together that year, even though we
weren't very much alike. Neither of us had other friends, that
could account for something. But sometimes I think we had
an unspoken respect for one another. I know I respected him,
anyway.

Raymond and I had a secret club to which only the two
of us belonged. The initiation consisted of pricking our
fingers and intermingling our blood in a vow of friendship.
Our club, like our friendship, was an antidote to the loneliness
of growing up in a small town like Scotia.

The Sproat family lived just down the street from us.
There was always trouble at his house. There was always

fighting. Raymond's mother, Fay, was an alcoholic. She existed in a haze of whiskey stupor. His father, Frank, worshipped the bottle, too. He started early every day and with each additional drink he turned increasingly angry.

Raymond was marked up every week or so. He wore constant bruises on his cheeks, and his eyes were sometimes swollen, and as colorful as a sunset. Once, when he got caught stealing five dollars from his mother's purse, his father punched him so hard he dislocated his jaw. Then he hit him again for good measure and bloodied his nose. After that he called Redwood Memorial Hospital and told them to come get his boy. Raymond spent a lot of time at that hospital. Once he had to have his broken arm set with a steel pin. Another time it took six stitches to close a cut over his eye.

Raymond's family lived in a dark pit of sadness and confusion, and they daily sunk deeper into that pit.

Beatings from his father did not stop Raymond from doing what he wanted. He was fearless, confident. He never backed away from trouble. I admired and envied that in him. I wanted to be more like Raymond because I was tired of being picked on. I was sick of bullies hawking snot on my shirt and then howling like monkeys when I tried to wipe it off. I had had enough of being taunted with nicknames like Dork Face or Ass Wipe whenever I walked past them.

My faith in Raymond was boundless. I remember riding down the steepest streets in town on the handlebars of his rusty old Schwinn bicycle. We flew down those streets. If we had hit a rock or a pothole I would have been ground into the pavement, probably splitting open my head in the process. But I wasn't worried. Raymond led me into danger many times, but he always led me out again.

Raymond's father worked at the sawmill where he yanked two hundred pound boards around as if they were teacups. He had a deep scar on one cheek and another on his forehead that said he was no stranger to either pain or bloodshed. Frank operated on a notable short fuse. When he was angry, he started punching, and he didn't care who was watching. One day he showed up at our school, dirty, and half-crazed with whiskey and rage. He had a baseball bat in his hand, and he told the teacher that he was going to beat some sense into his worthless son or beat him to death. If Raymond was scared, he didn't show it. He just sat there laughing with the rest of us until the teacher finally drove his drunken father away.

That wasn't the end of it, not for Raymond, anyway. When he got home that evening, his father was waiting. He pulled Raymond inside and slammed the door, but it did little to muffle the noise. I walked home alone. By the time I reached the end of the block, I could still hear the shouting and crying. I was amazed at how far anger and sadness could travel.

Raymond and I did some wild things together. Sometimes we would hop aboard a lumber train headed south and ride it for several miles, with the stink of diesel exhaust sweeping back into our faces. Other times we would steal candy from the store, or play in the town graveyard, toppling the tombstones and rolling the big granite cylinders downhill. Alone, I would have never have had the courage to do such things. But with Raymond I felt safe, even in the graveyard when it got dark.

One day, in an act of imitation of our parents' lives, we shared a bottle of whiskey in the woods.

It was the first week of September. The weather was unseasonably cold and damp. A drab cloak of low clouds had swallowed the town and sunk down against the earth itself. I woke early, tugged on my jeans and T-shirt and headed for Raymond's house. When I got there the front door was open, but I didn't go inside. I waited on the porch and peeked through the window.

In the small apartment both light and shadow loomed with an unguessable violence. Crumpled papers and beer cans littered the floor. Cigarette butts overflowed in the ashtrays. On the red Formica table in the living room, empty whiskey bottles were strewn about like bled cats. Fay was awake. She was in the kitchen throwing up, emptying her stomach for another day of drinking. Frank was awake, too. From the bedroom came the sound of his voice.

"You act like a good for nothing punk," he shouted. "When are you going to grow up?"

"What did I do?" asked Raymond.

"You act like a real wise guy."

"Tell me what I did."

"One jerk-off remark after another. You'd better pull yourself together, you hear?"

"Yes."

"Yes, *what?*" said Frank.

"Yes, sir."

"Then do it."

The front door swung open and Raymond came strolling out, grinning, and holding a bottle of Coke. His father caught wind of the smile, spun him around, and back-handed him. The force of his blow sent the Coke bottle spinning across the porch, spewing its contents. Raymond's mother stepped between them.

"Stop," she screamed.

"I'll beat him until he's black and blue," Frank yelled, pushing her aside.

Raymond stepped forward. "Leave her alone."

His father shut him up with one furious motion of his hand, a quick punch that sent Raymond sprawling to the floor.

"I'll take care of your smart ass once and for all." Frank loomed over him, fists doubled. Raymond dodged around his father and sprinted off the porch, blood trickling from one side of his mouth. He wasn't crying, but the corners of his eyes were prickling with it. Frank staggered forward and spotted me.

"What are you doing here?" he shouted. I could see waves of anger all around him in wiggly lines.

"Waiting for Raymond," I said.

Frank winced. He was insulted that I had replied. That I had spoken at all. He came nearer, dangerous with unexpended wrath. "Wait somewhere else. Get lost."

I stepped back and the door slammed. For long moments I stood there, imagining revenge. I magnified myself in years, strength, confidence, and nerve. I whipped Raymond's father with my tongue until he cried and begged my pardon for all he had ever done against his son. Then I made him

69

stand to one side while I broke his whiskey bottles, and he was knee deep in shattered glass.

Raymond came out of hiding. There was a bruise on his bottom lip and his eyes were swollen. He was fighting desperately to keep his dignity.

"Let's get out of here," he said.

"Where should we go?" I asked, but he didn't answer. With Raymond leading we headed east, toward the edge of town. By then I knew where we were going.

Our clubhouse was located deep in a forest of second growth redwoods. The trees were thick there, with branches coming almost to the ground in many places. There was no path leading to our clubhouse. It was well concealed, hidden away in the thicket. The place was little more than a few planks nailed together to keep out the weather, but it was ours. It was where went to smoke pilfered cigarettes and to be alone. We walked through the thicket without speaking, pushing our way through a tangle of salal and blackberry vines.

At one point Raymond stopped and pointed to his jacket: "Hey, Cole," he said. "Check this out." The metal tip of a flat bottle protruded from a side pocket.

"What is it?" I asked.

Raymond laughed. "What do you think?" He pulled out the bottle and held it up for me to see. "It's whiskey. I copped it off my old man."

"What are we gonna do with it?"

He laughed again. "We're gonna drink it."

I must have made a face because Raymond looked at me and said, "You're not chicken, are you?" I nodded. I never thought of lying to Raymond. He cuffed me on the shoulder lightly. "Don't be scared. Booze can't hurt you."

I nodded again, satisfied. He smiled and took off, climbing up the hill with me in hot pursuit.

Halfway up the ridge it began to rain. Thunder whacked and cracked. Lightning flashed so close that I could smell it, and not far away there was a splintering, rending sound as a tree fell. The wind bucked and buffeted.

We reached the clubhouse, bellied down, and crawled in through the tiny entrance. It was damp and dark inside, and laced with a myriad of spider webs that clung to my face. With a wave of my hand I brushed them aside, shuddering at the thought of a spider making tracks along my neck.

Raymond removed the bottle from his jacket, unscrewed the cap and took a long drink. He handed the bottle to me.

"Try it," he said. "You never tasted anything like it in your life. Tastes like fire." Bravely, feeling privileged and adult, I took the bottle and raised it to my mouth. Raymond held my elbow. "A small sip," he said. "It's real strong."

I took a deep breath, slugged down some whiskey, and felt my eyes fill with water. It scalded all the way down. I coughed and my nose ran.

Raymond thumped me on the back. "What do you think? Pretty good, huh?"

"Yeah," I croaked. I wanted to like the whiskey, to share in the pleasure of it with Raymond, but my stomach was burning and my arms were beginning to tingle. Raymond swigged at the bottle again, his cheeks bulging and bubbles rising in the whiskey as he drank. Then he handed it back to me. Going down this time it burned a little less. My whole body was warm.

"Feel anything yet?" he asked. I drank again, deeply, and some of the whiskey trickled down my chin and onto my shirt.

"Almost," I said. "I think, maybe." For long moments we sat sheltered, passing the bottle back and forth. I leaned against the wall of the clubhouse, trying to decide whether everything around me seemed different because of the whiskey, or just because everything truly was different.

"How you feeling now?" he asked.

"No pain," I told him, and it was purely the truth. Outside, rain came down in great whistling cataracts, whipped into a spray by a cold northern wind. The storm enveloped me, like a lover breathing in my ear.

"We can drink all the time when we grow up," Raymond said, stirring me from my reverie. I leaned into his certainty as if it gave off heat. Sitting there I thought about being an adult and of leaving our town, of starting a life of my own. When I thought of those things, with the whiskey in my stomach and the rain beating down just out of reach, I was happy and the world was suddenly a place of love and peace. I rested my chest against my folded legs and touched my forehead to the rough surface of a board. A hand settled on my shoulder.

"You okay?"

I nodded. "Yeah." I would have said more, but I couldn't get my lips to move. My mouth was stuffed with cotton. Raymond, on the other hand, appeared to be fine. He was sharp, coherent. The whiskey seemed to have no effect on him.

"Can you make it home?" he asked.

I glanced out through a crack in the wall. The rain had stopped and the sky had taken on a clarity that made my eyes ache. Water dripped from every tree.

"Sure," I said. "No problem."

"All right," Raymond said. "Gotta go, daddy-o. See you around." He crawled out the entrance, brushed off his pants, and moved easily and gracefully down the hill, humming to himself. As if he didn't have a care in the world. As if he was going to someplace real neat, instead of back to a small, dingy apartment with two alcoholic parents.

Later I stumbled out of the woods, pushing my way through the brush and low branches that stuck out from the trees like men's arms.

At home I threw up in the toilet. My mother called, "Are you okay?" I didn't answer. I went to my room. She came in a few minutes later asked me what I was doing in bed at eight o'clock on a Saturday night.

"I don't feel good," I told her. She put her hand on my forehead.

"No fever," she said. "But you do look awful."

Sleep didn't come easy that night. When it did, it was fragmented at best. My brain was filled with half thoughts, pieces that didn't seem to fit, dreams that made no sense.

The next morning, head throbbing, I headed for Raymond's house. He was waiting for me. The second I knocked on the door he jumped out and tackled me. We rolled around on the porch for a minute. Then he let me up.

"I thought of something cool," he said. "Real cool."

"What is it?" I asked. When Raymond told me, I was shocked. He wanted to set fire to an old, abandoned house on Diekman Lane. It was a stupid, crazy thing to do, but that was Raymond. He had set fire to things before: Dry grass, haystacks, and outhouses. Then he would crouch in the shadows and watch the fire department roll in to battle the blaze. When he suggested burning down the house, I was frightened. I knew he meant to go through with it.

"Come on," he said, "are you in or not?"

I wanted to tell him no. I wanted to explain that what he had planned was wrong, and that we could get into big trouble over it. But the last thing I wanted to do was lose Raymond's friendship.

"Okay," I said, "I'm in."

He clapped me on the back. "Race you," he said, making our mission of crime sound light-hearted, like we were running to the store for a soda pop.

"No way," I said. "I'll wax you."

"When I say go.

"When you're ready."

"Go."

Raymond and I raced through town, past the drugstore where we bought cherry smashes, past the post office, past our school where cardboard snowmen and construction paper reindeer were beginning to appear in windows. We ran along, faster and faster, our sneakers digging up gravel, our bodies leaning out ahead of our blue-jeaned legs. Off into the countryside, headed for trouble.

Chapter Seven

The house on Diekman Lane lay wreathed in blackberry vines and was partially collapsed in a spiral of timbers and twisted roof. Staring at it I felt a chill of panic creep over me. I stood rooted to the spot, but Raymond didn't hesitate. He walked right up and pushed open the door. Then he slid open a book of matches, took one out, and raked it across the striker. My heart trip hammered with fear as he threw the match into a pile of old clothing. The floor of the house was instantly enveloped in flame.

I had never seen a real fire before, and I was surprised by how swift and unpredictable it seemed. Through a broken window I could see flames shooting up to the ceiling. The scent of the smoke, when the wind blew it toward us, made my eyes and nose water. I could hardly believe what was happening. Maybe I'll become a criminal, I though. Maybe I'll go to prison for the rest of my life.

We watched the fire barrel into itself for a while, long enough to get a little drunk on it. Suddenly Raymond ran into the house. He plunged through the smoke and quivering arms of flames, and slammed the door shut behind him.

"Raymond," I yelled, chasing after him. I could hear him shouting, loud curses, banshee screams. The door was locked. I pounded on the walls, which were already warm. "Raymond," I cried again. "Open the door." I began to panic. There was nothing to stop the fire with. No hose, no extinguisher, nothing. I kicked at the door, trying to knock it off its hinges.

I didn't know what to do. I was rummaging in the yard for something to break down the door when it flew open and Raymond stumbled out. Smoke wisped off him. His face was streaked by soot and his hair was singed on one side.

"Man," he said, "that was *cool.*"

"Are you crazy?" I yelled. "What were you doing in there?" He spit a wad of blackened phlegm.

"Whoo*ee*," he replied. "You should have seen the inside of that place." Then he looked at me. "What? You thought I wasn't coming out?" My heart pounded. The air in front of the house seemed to wiggle and fray.

"Why'd you go back in?" I asked.

He shrugged. "I don't know. I guess I wanted to see what it was like." I stood stunned for a moment. Behind us the flames roared and crackled. In the distance a siren wailed, growing steadily louder.

"Here they come," Raymond said, pulling me by the arm. "Let's split." Then he dragged me away into the forest before the fire trucks arrived.

That was Raymond, a week before his death in an hour so alive with energy I will never forget it.

The following Tuesday was the start of deer season, and Raymond wanted to go hunting. Another kid at school offered to take him. The boy's parents owned a cabin in the mountains south of town and hunted there often. It was the opportunity of a lifetime, a chance to get away from school and maybe even shoot a deer.

Raymond didn't own a rifle but his father did. It was a .30-06 caliber with a 3x9 power scope. He kept it cocked and loaded in the back of his closet. Raymond swiped the rifle on the day he was to go hunting. He took it without asking. Just like that.

The next few days dragged by. I was bored and lonely without Raymond around. Then, on Friday afternoon, Teddy Waterston came running up the street.

"Hey, did you hear what happened?" he said, "Your friend's dead."

"What?" I said. At first I didn't understand.

"He's dead," said Teddy. "My mom told me at lunchtime. No lie. Your buddy, Raymond, is dead."

The story, or what Teddy's mother had heard, was that Raymond had been shot while hunting. He and his friend had been walking down a hill with their guns when the other kid stepped into a hole and stumbled forward. As he fell, his rifle discharged and Raymond was hit. The bullet entered just under his right arm and exited on the left side of his neck. He dropped to the ground, bleeding profusely. The other boy tried to stop the blood with his hands, but it burst out from the red lip of wound and flooded his wrists. The boy ran for help. Within minutes Raymond was gone.

All I could do was nod. Somehow, though, it didn't quite register. My thoughts drifted. I remembered the time a group of high school boys bet Raymond and me that we wouldn't cross the railroad bridge north of town.

It was a wood trestle with no rail, one hundred feet high and more than two hundred yards long, connecting the cut banks on either side of the river. The river itself was deep and swift. If you fell, or if a train came, you were finished. That was the dare, to get across.

It looked easy until I stepped onto the bridge and saw the river far below, I was instantly paralyzed by the height. But Raymond was leading the way, so I crept out on the bridge and looked straight ahead. There were wide spaces between the trestles and no railing to hang onto. I walked carefully, slowly, toward the other side. Wind moved my hair, my body. The smell of creosote flooded my nose. I kept sensing the beginnings of a fall, the feeling that comes just before you lose control.

I stopped mid-trestle. My feet became part of the bridge. I couldn't move. My breath came short. I was sure I was about to die, positive of it. Then I saw Raymond walking back to me, peaceful and natural.

"Come on, Cole," he said, "you can do it." His calmness flowed through me like rope. It ran the length of my legs and I continued to the other side of the tresses with Raymond.

Then, to show the others what we were made of, he ran back out to the middle of the bridge, climbed down, and hung from a crosstie by his hands.

"Man, that kid is crazy," said one boy. The others agreed.

But wasn't that what everyone said about Raymond? Wild as sunspots and dead at thirteen, and not one day in his short life wasted.

The funeral service was in a plain raw building set in the center of town. The walls were cinder block, and the light shining through the tall clear windows was bald and merciless. There were folding chairs instead of pews.

Raymond's parents sat in the front row. His father was beside himself with sorrow. You would have thought Raymond's death would hardly have merited a tear from him, or even a good-bye, but Frank was heart-broken. He draped himself over the casket, weeping. It took several men to wrench him away.

I can't remember what the minister said that afternoon. I probably didn't hear anything. I only remember passing in front of the coffin, staring at Raymond, and trying not to cry. They had dressed him in a dark blue suit and a white shirt and necktie. His hands were folded across his chest and his face was imperfectly rouged, like an old lady's. They had smoothed some kind of oil on his hair, but it wouldn't lie flat. I stared at him, thinking no one could lie so still for so long without moving. I waited for Raymond's eyelids to flutter, for his chest to move. His motionlessness was terrifying. I remember closing my eyes and whispering his name, begging, pleading for him to come back.

I went up into the woods after the funeral. The sky was clear. A cold breeze blew from the north. The wind was on my face and my arms, but I couldn't feel a thing. I walked up to the clubhouse and climbed inside. After I sat there for a while, I began to cry. The tears came up slowly, the way a spring fills, and brimmed over, and the first ones ran down my face and splashed warm on the back of my hands. I cried hard and for a long time. I was glad Raymond wasn't there to see me.

It was a sad year. I had lost my best friend and now felt rudderless, without direction. Then my mother was laid off at the mill and unable to find work. During that period there were no vacations or weekend outings for us. Movies and hot school lunches were out of the question. There was no money for anything other than rent and groceries. We passed from month to month, through the tides of that year, like a ship that was charting a course where the view was always familiar. Then one day everything changed. A new man fell from the sky and landed on our doorstep.

It happened on a winter day. The morning was brittle with cold. I heard a car pull into the driveway and peeked out the window. There was a blue Chevy pickup, motor idling, vapors rising in the jelled air. A man sat behind the wheel looking big and full of purpose. It was my new father. I had been told he was coming. He had married my mother a week before in Nevada. Then he had traveled to Southern California, to the home of his previous wife, to collect his tools and clothes.

I was choked with excitement. What would he think of me? My hair wasn't combed and I hadn't brushed my teeth. I was taken with a terrible idea. What if he had seen me already? What if he thought, this kid is too puny to make a decent son. A boy should be stronger and taller.

My mother called from the living room. I stuffed my shirttail into my pants, hollered "Yeah?" and straightened up erect, prepared to make the best impression possible. Then I opened my bedroom door and stepped into the living room. I stood there for a moment, speechless. There in the flesh was the father I had dreamed of in a thousand forms since I'd realized that other boys had a second parent, a parent who knew men's stuff and could pass it down to them.

He introduced himself. His name was Ernest McKenzie. He had bare looking green eyes, a gap between his top teeth, and hair as black as wrought iron that was combed with force off his forehead. His voice was rough, yet caressing, like the lick of a tomcat's tongue. He smelled of cigarette smoke and Old Spice cologne.

I rummaged for something to say. What should I say? "Hello, Father? Dad? Sir?" Should I hug him or shake hands? Oh why hadn't I combed my hair? He offered his hand and I shook it. His grip was meaty, muscular. He was, as I knew from a boy's curiosity and observation, unusually strong.

"How's the fishing around here?" he asked. I had no idea. I had never caught a fish in my life.

I shrugged, hardly daring to raise my eyes to his.

"How about the hunting?"

"I don't know," I lied. My lips were sealed about the hunting trip with Uncle Howard. I would never tell. I had made a promise.

Ernie fixed a cigarette on his bottom lip, snapped a little no-nonsense stainless steel lighter under it, and returned the lighter to the chest pocket of his shirt. The smoke rose up the right side of his face so he narrowed that eye.

"Well, we're just gonna have to find out," he said, and tipped me a wink. There had been a thrill in receiving that wink from him. It put the two of us in cahoots. It made us secret allies in a manly way. I chewed my lip and was silent for a moment. I was crazy with questions I wanted answered, but the idea of asking them embarrassed me, for to be so ignorant about such things seemed shameful.

My mother gave Ernie a tour of the house. I followed close behind. It didn't take long to show him around. Our house was small. It had the functional economy of a military barracks. There was a tiny kitchen, two cramped bedrooms, and a bathroom. That was the extent of it. When they were done Ernie pulled me aside and said, "Say, I got a hell of an idea. How would you like to go fishing tomorrow?"

"S-sure," I stammered. But—"

"No buts about it," he said. "I'll wake you in the morning." Then, he handed me a half dollar and asked me if I would run to the store for cigarettes. Camels were the brand he preferred. Would I run to the store for cigarettes? I would have circled the globe if he had requested it. I was falling all over myself getting out the door.

Already I liked everything about Ernie, the coarseness of his hair, his deep voice, his strength. His every gesture suggested a man of endless and exuberant energy. He seemed kind and caring too, the kind of man a boy needs around when he's growing up. If I was going to call anyone my father, this would be a good man to choose. I was just pulling out of the driveway on my bicycle when Ernie poked his head out the door.

"Get yourself a candy bar with the change," he shouted. The man is a God, I remember thinking, as I pedaled down the block toward the corner store.

As Ernie promised, he woke me at dawn the following morning to go fishing. On the porch I watched a pearly band in the east give way to a deepening flush of pink, and then rapidly brightening to a deep blue. We gathered up our fishing gear from the garage and headed out.

Ernie assured me there were trout, big speckled trout with bellies as red as cherry candy in the river. We climbed over fences and crossed stubble fields, our shoes cracking against the dry barley stalks. Excited, I took steps twice my normal stride. I was thinking of promised fish. Ernie carried his excitement lightly, the way a hunter carries a loaded shotgun over a fence.

By the time we reached the river, the sun was up. Rays of light, as pretty as a drawing in a child's Sunday school workbook, were shining through the trees and dappling the sand at our feet. The air was filled with the sweet, damp scent of water. Our fishing spot was a deep pool, just downstream from a long section of rapids.Ernie added sinkers and hooks to our lines. Then he threaded worms onto the hooks. A fish jumped from the blue water, flashing like quicksilver.

"See right there?" He pointed to the place where the trout had jumped. "Damn. She was a big one."

Ernie always called things she, but I couldn't tell how he knew. He said, "I guess she'll be a hot one today," or "It looks like she'll rain." Or when we were fishing: "Just skim the worm across the water and watch her jump."

I drew back and made my cast. "Did I get her in the right spot?" I asked.

"Just right," Ernie said. The line tightened and the current carried the worm into sight at the end of the pool. I could feel the sinkers tap tapping on the rocks. Suddenly, the tip of my pole dipped and the line straightened, taut as a wire. A bite! I reeled in and examined the hook. It was bare. I put on another worm and repeated my cast, exactly. The writhing pink worm vanished. Again the quick, hard pull. I jerked and reeled in my line. On the hook was a ten inch speckled trout, my first trout. I kept cool until I tried to take the hook out of his mouth. He was lying covered with sand on the little beach where I had landed him.

My hands were shaking, but finally I managed to pick him up and shout to Ernie: "Look. I got one."

"That's a beauty," he said, launching a terrific smile. "And it's the first catch of the day. You're turning out to be quite a fisherman."

I preened inward, murmuring my thanks. Ernie took a cigarette out of his shirt pocket and lit it. Smoke shot through his nose into the air. Then he picked up his pole and waded out knee deep into the river. On his first cast he hooked a fish, then another. He wasted no time catching a full stringer of trout.

When we had enough for supper, Ernie cleaned them in the riffles, letting water spill into their slit, flapping bellies and swirl about their pink gills. Then he arranged them in a basket between layers of grass and wild mint.

That evening my mother wrapped the trout in bread

crumbs, sprinkled on butter and lemon rind, and cooked them. If I had ever tasted better food, I don't know what it is.

The next time Ernie took me fishing it was at night, with a flashlight and a pitchfork. This kind of fishing was called gaffing and it always took place right after the first good rains of winter, when the steelhead moved upstream to spawn. Gaffing was against the law, but it was something I never questioned. Life in Scotia was simple and sometimes perilously close to impoverished and, as Ernie pointed out, food was food. A man with a pitchfork could easily kill a steelhead during spawning season and have enough for his family to eat for several days.

Chapter Eight

It was midnight and stars were scattered like spilled salt across the sky. We motored out of town and pulled onto a dirt road that ran through the lonely redwoods, bouncing along the bumps and dips. The truck rattled past swamps full of frogs that piped shrilly and, confused by our headlights, hopped giddily onto the road where they were squashed beneath our wheels.

"Are you ready?" Ernie asked, as we rattled down the potholed lane.

"Yes, sir," I said, trying hard to conceal my excitement. I was gripping the pitchfork so tightly I feared I would break it. "Do you think we'll get a fish tonight?"

"It'll be a miracle if we don't," he said.

We drove to the mouth of the Eel River, where the steelhead congregated just before their long journey upstream, and parked under a grove of trees. Ernie switched off the motor and stepped out into the darkness. I followed. The chilly air carried on its sleek back the sounds of night birds and the creaking of the trees above us.

At the river we came to an open place, a gravel beach. Then, despite the darkness, we dropped into a crouch and peered into the water. In the shallows I could see the dark, shiny backs of fish sticking out. Steelhead, fresh from the ocean. A big one rolled. Another shot through a riffle, fining upstream against the current.

Ernie signaled and I moved into the water. I was so excited I could barely hold onto the pitchfork. A fish came right at me. It tried to turn at the last second, but it was too late. I thrust the tines into the water and felt them hit flesh. Then I threw the steelhead on the bank, flopping and twisting. Its body was solid, and its teeth felt as sharp as a new saw blade. I was wet and shivering.

"That's one hell of a big fish," Ernie said, laughing. "I think I saw the water level drop a foot when you pulled it out."

I started laughing too. Then Ernie took the pitchfork and waded back into the water. As he fished, I sat on the bank staring at the steelhead, fixing that moment in my memory so it would stay with me forever.

It didn't take long to think of Ernie as a father. He was not blind or mean-spirited like other men I knew. He was hard, but in a different way. The way a baseball is hard under the scuffed leather. I enjoyed being with him. I liked how he made me feel. He never acted as though I didn't exist, as other grownups did. He treated me like I was good to have around, a boy who could help a man with a job.

Ernie was a carpenter. He had a big toolbox filled with woodworking tools. He cherished those tools and took excellent care of them. Just after he moved in Ernie set to work remodeling our house. It was something to see him plane a piece of wood, and watch it take shape with every peeling that curled from the blade. Sometimes he would ask me to hold a board for him, or bring him a tool.

"Wood is different from anything else," he said. "It requires care and respect. One slip of the saw, one shave too many with the plane, and your work is ruined. Fit only for burning."

Ernie wasn't proud or smug about his craft, but when he said he was going to make something you believed him. When he took a saw to a piece of wood his cuts were straight and even. Ends mated up. His nails went in flush. When Ernie joined two pieces of wood together they fit perfectly. He could make a door stand up plumb, and a window slide up and down as smooth as butter.

When there wasn't enough carpentry to keep him busy, Ernie hired on at the mill. He worked at the plywood plant, where he glued and patched 4x8 sheets of veneer and stacked it into neat units. He would finish each day covered with sweat and trailing the smell of glue and freshly-cut wood. There would be sawdust in the cuffs of his pants. Ernie never complained about the job, even though the pay was minimal and his back often gave him problems. And he was generous with the money he struggled so hard to make.

One Saturday I collected pop bottles to get twenty five cents to go to the movies. I later found out that the ticket price at the Bijou had gone up to fifty cents. I stomped back to the house, angry, kicking things.

Ernie had just finished a weekend shift at the mill and was still in his work clothes. He asked me what was wrong. When I told him, he reached in his pocket and pulled out a handful of sawdust and came up with two quarters. His fingers were blistered and cut open from the rough lumber. He handed me the money. It was probably the last he had. I hurried back to the movie—*The Blob*.

By the time I got home Ernie was already in bed. There was work early the next morning. I sneaked into his room and watched him sleep. I never woke him up to thank him. I just wanted to look at him, and think about the kind of father I had.

The good memories far outweigh the painful ones. But some memories huddle in a grainy light. They lodge in my mind like an old wound that never entirely healed. Ernie had a weakness for alcohol. He drank compulsively, secretly, in pain and trembling. And when he drank there was always trouble. Usually it happened on the weekends. He would start early Saturday morning and, by the time evening rolled around, he would be passed out in his recliner, an alcoholic darkness covering him like a black sheet.

All evening, until my bedtime, I would tiptoe past him, as past a snoring dragon. Then I curled fearfully in my sheets, listening, because eventually he would wake up, and the fighting would begin. My mother would sling accusations at him. Ernie would snarl back. Their voices clashed in the darkness. Before long she would retreat to their bedroom, sobbing, not from the blows of fists, for he never struck her, but from the force of his words.

Left alone, Ernie would prowl the house, thumping into furniture, rummaging in the kitchen and slamming doors. I would lie there hating him, loving him, fearing him, knowing that I had failed him. I told myself that he needed alcohol to ease the ache gnawing at his belly, the ache I must have caused by disappointing him somehow.

Sometimes Ernie would stop for a drink on the way home from work. When he got carried away, he would go on a binge that would last for days and cause great problems.

I came home from school one afternoon and immediately knew something was wrong. I could sense trouble as soon as I stepped onto the porch. I could smell it, feel it against my skin. My mother met me at the door. She looked uneasy, like all messengers with bad news.

"Ernie's been arrested," she said. And then she pulled her housecoat tight because there was a cold vein in the air, the kind of cold that would be on us for awhile. "He was picked up for driving under the influence."

He was in big trouble. It was Ernie's second drunk driving offense. This time he was going to jail. On the day he was sentenced my mother and I were there. Outside the courtroom we were allowed a few minutes with him. Ernie looked bad. He had several nights' growth of beard, matted hair, and bloodshot eyes. His face was gray from fatigue and epic drinking.

"You'll be the man of the house, Cole," he told me. "I want you to take care of everything."

"Yes, sir," I said. My throat tightened and tears came to my eyes. I didn't want to cry in front of him, and to check myself I pushed at the gap between my front teeth with my tongue.

"Don't let me down now, hear?" He smiled, but it looked manufactured. As he was escorted away by a deputy sheriff, I told myself I would never let him down, no matter what.

Time moved slowly, sluggishly. A month without Ernie seemed like an eternity. For the first few weeks my mother was deeply depressed. She slept late, something she had never done before. When I came home from school, I sometimes found her still in her bathrobe, sitting at the kitchen table and staring dazedly out the window. In the silence of the house my mother battled her depression, moving beneath its weight like some lethargic creature at the bottom of the sea. I tried to keep busy by immersing myself in schoolwork and chores. It was the only way I could escape being drawn deeper into my own unhappiness.

Somehow we made it through that month, and after Ernie's release from jail there was peace for a time. He went back to work at the mill and kept busy around the house. He even tried to stop drinking, but for Ernie that was like trying to plug the holes in a poorly constructed earthen dam. As soon as you got one leak stopped, a new one sprung up someplace else. It was not the end of our troubles. It was only the beginning of more hard times.

The bullies never disappeared either, they just had different names. In high school there was a gang of thugs who enjoyed beating up on other kids. Tony Albers was their self proclaimed leader. He wore a leather jacket and had a flat top cut so close you could see his scalp, pale as a potato. Tony and his gang loitered in the hallways, tripping students and slamming their heads against lockers. I was one of their favorite victims.

Encounters with Tony and his gang usually began with

a slighting remark and ended in a flurry of fists. They would spit on me and pull on my shirt until the seams ripped. When they were feeling especially mean-spirited they would work me over good.

One Friday I came home with a black eye. After supper Ernie called me into the living room.

"Put some ice on that eye and it'll be okay," he said. Later he took me outside. He was going to teach me how to fight.

"Leave him alone," my mother said. "Don't you think he's had enough for one day?"

"He's never been taught to defend himself," Ernie said. "He's got to learn to fight or they'll always be boys coming at him." Ernie believed that it was a man's place in life to take punishment and give back more than he took. That's what a father had to teach his son.

So I learned to fight. That evening I was instructed to tighten my fists hard, to strike out straight from the shoulder and never punch backing up. Ernie showed me how to stand, how to cut a jab by snapping my fist inward, and how to guard myself by keeping my chin low. He taught me how to put my weight behind a punch.

"Fly all over your man," he said. "A good fighter is one who will slip under a punch and give two in return. When a man makes you take off your coat, you've got to teach him a lesson. One he won't forget."

"Will I be able to defend myself?" I asked.

"Only if you're tough," he said.

The following day at school, during lunch, Tony Albers came up behind me and pushed me to the ground. I went full length onto the pavement. I got up and shoved him back. He started to laugh, it was almost a giggle. Then he turned suddenly angry.

"That was stupid," he said. "Now I'm gonna beat the crap out of you."

This time I was ready for Tony. I slipped under his fist and delivered a right to his nose. There was a lifetime of injustice behind my punch. Bone crunched. Blood streamed from his nostrils into his cupped hands. His face filled with stunned surprise.

"Damn you," he cried. "I'll kill you for that."

"Knock his brains out," yelled one of his friends. A knot of onlookers closed around us. Tony rushed at me, arms flailing, fists raining on my shoulders. I surprised myself by landing one on his eye. He stopped and roared. The eye was already closing up. His face had gone scarlet, his nostrils streamed. Tony wasn't used to having someone fight back. He was throwing wild punches. I danced in and out, making him strike air again and again.

"Stand still," he gasped. Tony charged me. I feinted to the left, just as Ernie had showed me. When he shifted to meet the feint, I put everything I had into a haymaker that caught Tony's chin and snapped his head around. Fire bloomed in my knuckles.

He made no noise, not even a whimper. His legs buckled and he dropped to the pavement. When Tony got up, he was crying. Hard, angry tears. I saw blood in his teeth, like a smear of food dye. Nobody offered to help him, not even his friends. Somebody laughed. Another kid said, "Go home, crybaby. Go home to mama."

It was the last time I was ever bothered by Tony Albers.

One Saturday Ernie wanted to take me hunting, but my mother wouldn't have it. She made a face as though she had bitten into a sour apple, and gave a brusque shake of the head.

"It's too dangerous," she said, "I don't want you going."

"You let me go with Uncle Howard," I whined.

"That was target practice," she said. "You didn't go hunting, did you?"

"No," I said. I bit my tongue, thinking how I had almost spilled the beans.

For the rest of the day I moped about the yard, waiting impatiently for my mother to change her mind, injecting a "please?" one moment and a "why not?" the next, hoping beyond hope to wear her down. Finally, her face flamed with anger. She slammed a frying pan down on the counter. Utensils slid to the floor. Tears sprang to her eyes and she put a hand over her mouth to hold back a cry of anguish.

"Go on, then," she said, her hand dropping to the collar of her sweater and fiddling there, as it often did when she was upset. "Go, I don't care. No one around here listens to me anyway." Then she went into her bedroom and shut the door. It was the only place in the house where she could get away from men and their talk of guns and hunting.

It was a cold, clear morning when Ernie and I set out in the truck. The wind rushed through the rolled down window and brushed its cold wrist against my cheek.

Ernie exhaled cigarette smoke slowly, through his nostrils, and it was swept away from his face. I could smell the whiskey on him and the odor of sweat. In his jacket he looked bulkier than ever, and unbreakable, like a redwood stump left over from the loggers.

I was holding his deer rifle, a .30-30 to which was clamped a 3X to 9X variable scope. It was as heavy as rocks. When I pushed the rifle on fire there was a red spot on the safety. My heart beat faster every time I saw that crimson slot flash before my eyes. I had a feeling that something very important was about to happen, that this would be an evening to remember.

"You ready with that gun, Cole?" he asked.

"Yes, sir."

"Not a little nervous about shooting a deer?"

"No, sir," I lied.

"Well, you should be," Ernie said. "Hunting is serious. It should never come easy. A man never kills anything without good reason. You understand?"

"I think so. But I'm not afraid to kill a deer."

"I'm not saying you are or that you should be. The deer has to die so we can eat. That's why we hunt. But you should feel something. It comes from inside of you, and it's like saying you're sorry. Just not with words. If it weren't for food we wouldn't be out here. We wouldn't be hunting."

"Yes, sir," I said, but I still wasn't quite sure what he meant. We passed a field that bordered the road and a farmhouse. The forest beyond seemed like breath drawn back.

A few miles down the highway Ernie slowed and hooked a right onto a narrow, twisting, gravel road. The truck went strumming over a cattle guard, and soon we were climbing a ridge covered with second-growth redwoods.

"You know," he said, "even if we don't get a deer tonight it's still good to be out here. Good to get away from the house." Ernie pulled a bottle of whiskey out from behind the seat and took a long drink. "That's what the woods are all about. It's where the women don't want to go."

Chapter Nine

We drove for a few more miles and crept around a tree-shrouded bend. Beyond it was a small clearing. Ernie stopped the truck.

"Look," he whispered, "down in that draw."

At first I could see nothing but shadow. Then I spotted the deer. It was watching us carefully, perfect in the moment of innocence and wonder. One large ear turned slowly toward us. Its black nose quivered with each breath.

"I see it." I whispered my reply since I did not want anything to be ruined because of what I said or did.

"Go ahead," he said. "You do it."

At first I thought I had misunderstood him. Then he reached over and twisted the handle on my door, quietly, so as not to spook the deer. I could hardly believe it. He wanted to give me the first shot.

I got out of the truck, slowly. The air was sharp-toothed. It bit my cheeks, nipped my chin. My hands were numb from the cold venom of countless bites.

"Aim for the chest," Ernie whispered. "That's the killing spot."

I nodded and brought the gun up to my shoulder, trying to line up the peep sight with the deer's neck. My pounding heart drove the gun in circles around the animal. A branch snapped. Through the sights I saw the deer look up, ears high and straining. It was about to bound away. I exhaled slowly and squeezed the trigger. I remember distinctly the report of the gun and the flash of the muzzle. The deer seemed to sink into the ground, hind legs first. Then, still straining to keep its head up, as if that alone would save it, the animal collapsed in the grass.

"Good shot," Ernie cried, clapping me on the back. "You got her."

For a second I was dazed, not quite understanding what had happened. Then I set down the gun and sprinted to the place where the deer had stood. It lay on its side, one leg twitching. There was a smear of blood on its chest. Its eyes were open, but it looked as if they were staring in instead of out.

"It's still alive," I said. My words were instantly translated into warm gouts of steam. Ernie pulled out his knife, the blade shining in the light.

"Watch how I do this," he told me, "because next time you have to field dress your own animal." Ernie reached down, put one arm around the deer's neck, raised his pocketknife and cut the jugular vein. Thick red blood poured out over his hands. It kept coming. There was a lot of it.

When there was no further struggle Ernie removed his jacket and shirt and got busy. Working quickly, he split the hind tendons, threaded them with a heavy branch, and hoisted the animal to the low limb of a nearby tree. Then he made a long incision through the skin, working it back with his fingers before making the second cut through the warm membrane. The steamy innards rolled out onto the ground, unbroken.

When Ernie was done, he rose and painfully stretched. I remember him standing there, stripped to the waist, covered with blood, telling me to be careful with the bladder, and to never let the hair touch the meat. But the most important thing he told me was that a man never backs away from doing what is necessary, no matter how unpleasant the job.

Later that year I learned to drive. It was in Ernie's pickup. One afternoon he said, "Here, take the keys and go up on Blue Line."

I had sat beside him many times, holding the wheel. Driving wouldn't be that hard, I thought. I climbed in and cranked over the engine. The interior smelled strongly of sun-warmed leather and gasoline fumes. The broken speedometer registered a petrified twenty five. Rain streaks and crushed insects blurred the windshield, one section of which was shattered in a bursting star pattern. The pickup was old, but it ran well. I put it in gear and pulled away from the house.

The Blue Line was a logging road that cut between Pacific Lumber Company land to the south, and the river to the north. That day I drove with courage and no skill. The Chevy pulled to the left and right, and I over-steered to compensate, trying to manage all those things, clutch, brake, wheel and shift knob.

I made it down the road without incident. When I reached the intersection of the main highway, I turned around and headed back, smiling from ear to ear. I had conquered the world. I knew that the two wheels of my Huffy bicycle would no longer be enough to satisfy my wanderlust.

Not long after that I took the truck for another drive. Pulling out of the driveway I was abruptly halted by a fencepost. I went back in the house and found Ernie in the kitchen having a morning cigarette.

"What's wrong?" he asked, his green eyes searching my troubled face.

"I creased the fender," I managed to say.

"You did what?"

"Creased the fender." He looked puzzled and followed me out to the garage. There he solemnly inspected the damage. I awaited his wrath.

Instead he said, "Don't worry. I was thinking on having that old truck painted anyway."

Thus did I find acceptance of my mistakes, as well as love and recognition. As I grew up, I learned that I must give to others what had been given to me. Ernie taught me that. He taught me a lot of things before I graduated from high school, important things that a man should know.

A week later the clouds closed over our family again. Ernie began to drink heavily. He was now drunk every day, spinning out of control like a car without brakes or steering. I wanted to tell him that I was worried. I was afraid he was killing himself, and that it had to stop. He had to give up drinking. But how do you say those things to someone you respect so deeply?

One Friday evening Ernie didn't come home from

work. My mother stood at the kitchen window for hours, watching for his pickup. It was just after midnight when the police finally called. Ernie had been in an accident. He was in the hospital. The officer said he had been driving like a blind man and was so messed up on whiskey he must have been pretty near blind at that. He had hit a utility pole and was ejected from his vehicle. In my mind, I saw his pickup smashed deliberately into a telephone pole. What shocked me as much as anything was suddenly realizing that I'd expected it. My mother and I rushed to the hospital.

Ernie was lucky. He had totaled his pickup, but he suffered only a slight concussion, a few broken ribs, and some bruised muscles. He would be okay. However, as soon as his injuries were mended, he would be sent back to jail. On top of that, there was an $800 fine to pay. This was high drama for our family. We didn't have that kind of money. And with Ernie not working, where would we get it?

"What's going to happen to us?" my mother cried. "Dear God." But God wasn't having any of it. He had long ago washed his hands of our family.

The next few months were a constant struggle for us, a fight for survival. My mother went back to work at the mill. I got a job after school changing irrigation pipe for a rancher. All the money we made went to paying off the fine. Twice a week we drove to the county jail to visit Ernie. My mother felt it was important to spend as much time together as we could, to remain a family. But even this did not help, because the family we set out to imitate did not really exist.

After Ernie had served his time in jail, the judge ordered him to attend AA meetings with the other human ships wrecked on the rocks which border the sea of alcohol. The meetings didn't help. Nothing seemed to help. Ernie went right back to drinking, never precisely remembering the bouts of drunkenness, his mind drawing a merciful curtain over each one as soon as it was over.

"How bad was it?" he would ask the morning after. "How much trouble did I get into?"

It was always that way when he was in the grip of alcohol. Even when he was conscious, he never seemed to be exactly inside of himself. Much of the time he seemed to be floating above his own head, like a helium filled balloon.

Then high school graduation, and boyhood was over. I was seventeen. A new path lay ahead, not through the woods, but to the military, and to a country about which I knew little. American men were fighting a war, and Marine Corps recruiters descended on our high school like a plague of locust. They marched about straight and tall in their khaki uniforms, their trousers holding a lethal crease, their shirts adorned with the ribbons of countless exotic battles.

During those final weeks of school, the recruiters came into our classrooms where they extolled the virtues of fighting for democracy, and spoke of honor and glory and the pride that came with being an American fighting man.

The Marines gathered a loyal following among the youth of Scotia. Why not? They were the toughest, the best. And they were proving it in a place called Vietnam.

The war found its way into our home each evening at about dinner time. In the course of a meal we would witness an intense ground battle in Dong hoi or a high altitude bombing raid over Ha tinh, or the napalming of some small village with an equally strange name.

And the soldiers were all young. The basic ingredients of the sixties, drugs, rock 'n' roll and the war, all came together on the television screen in some dark alchemy: Teenagers at war.

For me Vietnam seemed to be more about growing up than combat. It took on a mystical importance, eating its way like acid into my brain. I saw myself in a uniform with medals on my chest, a man who drove headlong to his death without even changing his expression. The Marines would be a heroic challenge against which I could test my manhood. Many of my friends had already signed up. If I waited much longer the war would be over.

Ernie's attitude toward my plan was a strange mixture of pride and faint alarm. He knew that I wasn't college material. My grades were indifferent to poor. My test scores for general aptitude showed that I wasn't very apt at anything. But he did not want me in the Marines.

Ernie was fifteen when he lied about his age and enlisted in the Navy. He had watched the Marines storm the beaches of Iwo Jima, and seen them fall like dominoes under Japanese fire until the sands were carpeted with blood and bodies. Ernie was patriotic, but he could not bear to send me off to Vietnam in a Marine uniform.

"Fighting for your country is one thing," he said, "dying

for it is another. Join the Navy. They'll teach you a decent trade."

"But I want to be part of the real war," I said. "I want to win medals." I had developed a keen desire for the insignias of honor, such as the decorations the Marine recruiters sported on their uniforms.

Ernie walked into his bedroom. From the corner of a closet he withdrew several dozen small blue boxes and laid them on the bed. When the medals had been removed from their dusty containers and laid out for inspection, I was rendered speechless. They were beautiful.

"Where did you get them?" I asked. I hadn't known that Ernie was a war hero. He had never once talked about it. That night I got the whole story. He was a veteran of WW II, a Navy man who had known the horror of having a ship sunk out from under him, twice. The first ship, the U.S.S. Bismark Sea, was hit in broad daylight and most of the men were rescued before the vessel had time to slip to the bottom.

The second ship was the one that gave him nightmares. The U.S.S. Indianapolis, a heavy cruiser, was sunk by two Japanese torpedoes shortly after transporting components of the atomic bomb to the island of Titian. The ship went down within minutes, along with 400 of its crew. The Indianapolis had been observing radio silence, so no one other than the crew of the Japanese submarine knew their location.

For five days 797 men were stranded in the Pacific Ocean with little more than life jackets. By the time they were rescued only 317 men remained. Many had died of exhaustion, exposure, and wounds inflicted when the ship was torpedoed. Others were victims of shark attacks. During those five days the waters around the men remained a constant crimson. The sharks fed non stop, day and night, darting into their dwindling numbers with speed and fury, ripping at dangling limbs with savage hunger. Ernie was one of the fortunate few who survived the harrowing ordeal. There were 880 other sailors who weren't as lucky.

He spent the remainder of that evening going over exciting sea battles and hair-raising kamikaze attacks. Ernie assured me that if I joined the Navy, I would see plenty of action. I could also pick up a useful trade for when I got out of the service. The Marines, on the other hand, would take me nowhere in the race for bread and butter.

"And one more thing," Ernie pointed out with a sly wink. "Women go crazy over a man in a sailor uniform." That did it. That sold me on becoming a sailor. So during the giddy days of John F. Kennedy's "New Frontier" I patriotically enlisted in the U.S. Navy.

Such were the decisions that shaped young lives during those impressionable years.

I discovered that I hated the military. It was a dispassionate and cold machine. I went to Vietnam, but I saw little action. Ernie had been right about one thing, though. I was safe. For a full year our ship patrolled the Gulf of Tonkin, shelling villages and shooting down enemy aircraft that dared to venture too close. Not once in that year did anyone return fire.

With the Marines it was a more deadly game. Foot soldiers became men in Vietnam. Men became dead, zipped up in green vinyl bags, shipped home, and buried with a twenty-one gun salute.

The war went by in a blur, and after I finished my sentence I came home. When I saw Ernie, I was shocked. In my absence a heart attack had taken its toll on him. His weight had dropped to 125 pounds. His hair was thinning, his complexion sallow. His quick grace had slowed to measured, halting steps intermittently punctuated by coughing breathlessness. He had lost his luminous glow. It was fading out of him by slow degrees until there would be no more of it.

Ernie was dying and it scared and enraged me. It seemed to me that when a person went it should be a quick thing. His heart was doing more than killing him, it was degrading him, demeaning him. But nothing, I found, not even a failing heart could keep him down.

That first week home I decided to go fishing. A storm had blown down from the north, whistling in as suddenly as a gunslinger's draw and with all out fury. The storm brought with it the first winter rain. I was elated, for fresh rain meant fresh steelhead. That evening, when I pulled on my rain slicker, Ernie struggled out of his recliner.

"I'm coming along," he said.

"No, you're not," my mother told him. "You're too sick to go out."

Ernie's face took on an expression of determination and willpower, something that firmed his chin and put fire back into his eyes.

"This might be my last chance to get a fish," he said, struggling to catch his breath. "I'm sure as hell not going to pass it up because I'm sick."

"Listen to the weather," I said. Rain pawed loudly on the roof. It chattered at the windows and streamed against the walls, its fingers weeping to get in.

"I don't care about the weather," he said, "I'm coming along."

Ernie wanted desperately to fish. He was going and that was that.

It was raining hard as we drove toward the river, a vertical down pour from a churning, blurry sky. Our headlights raked the stormy sky. Windshield wipers brushed the rain in a rhythmic bright wrap. We reached the river and parked. Ernie finished his cigarette, drawing the abrasive smoke in deep with a reverse whistle. Then he slowly climbed out of the truck and headed toward the river, flashlight and pitchfork in hand. I followed along behind. Rain was plucking leaves from the trees and turning stone gullies into streams. I had to breathe through my mouth to keep water out of my nose. I watched Ernie struggle along the path in little sudden gasps, like the desperate heaves of a bird caught in the chimney. At one point he stopped and leaned heavily on the pitchfork.

"Do you hurt?" I asked, crouching beside him. He had little breath for speaking, and shook his head no.

"Sure you don't want to go back home?" A vigorous head shake again.

We continued on. A few hundred yards down the trail

we eased over a bank to the soft sand of the river bar. Ernie was having trouble. His legs didn't want to respond smoothly to his mind's commands. From his coat pocket he produced a pint of whiskey. He uncapped the bottle and drank in long swallows. There was less than half a bottle remaining after his unbroken guzzle.

"You got to stay as wet on the inside as you are on the outside, so you won't warp," he said.

By the time we reached the river, the rain had let up and leveled out to its usual winter pace, not so much a rain as a dreamy smear that wiped over the land instead of falling on it. The river was swift and dark. You could hear the rocks moving under it with a muffled, blocky sound. Ernie took a cigarette out of his shirt pocket and turned out of the wind to light it.

"I hope we don't get a wet ass and no fish," he said.

With my flashlight I scanned the rapids and found nothing. Then, I pointed the light to the broad tailout of a pool and whistled softly at what I saw.

"Look, there they are," I said.

"Lordy, lordy," Ernie whispered. A smile brightened his face. "I bet there's at least a hundred fish out there." The steelhead were lying stock still, their backs out of the water. Though seemingly motionless, every so often one of them would shoot upstream, its tail fining against the current like river weed.

Ernie upended the bottle again, and the muscles of his throat worked in rapid convulsions. Then he grabbed the pitchfork and waded out into the water.

"Let's get busy," he said.

Ten yards from where he waded, a steelhead swirled. A few steps, a quick jab, and the fish was impaled on the end of his pitchfork, fighting vigorously.

"Damn thing must go twelve, fourteen pounds," he puffed, holding it in the air.

"It's a beauty," I said.

"Hoooeee, I feel good." He threw back his head, and howled like a dog cutting a hot trail. Silent lightning zigzagged miles away, followed by a crawling thunder roll. The storm was moving away.

Thirty minutes later the rain had ceased completely. The moon found holes in the clouds with skilled agility, making the river glisten with frost. Ernie and I continued to fish. Owls were flying that night, somewhere off in the woods, shrieking to start their prey.

Ernie finished one pint of whiskey and started on a second. He wiped his forehead and watched the sweat drip from the ends of his fingers.

"Boy, that's pure bourbon whiskey running off my hand."

The wind flicked my hair and cooled my scalp. I experienced a rowdy euphoria and a sudden love for the night, for the wind smelling of river, and for Ernie. We laughed at the sight of one another. Nothing funny had happened. It was just that kind of night, the kind that should never end.

Eventually, though, it did come to an end. Ernie was worn out. It became an effort for him to even lift his feet.

"Let's head home," I said.

He nodded. "Good idea. I think my bones have turned to lead."

I put the steelhead on a rope stringer and hoisted them to my shoulder. We stumbled back to the truck, slowed by the weight of the fish. On the way Ernie stopped many times to rest or to bubble the whiskey bottle.

"Let's sit down a minute," he said at one point. "I'm so tired, I almost fell ass over cowcatcher there." He collapsed onto the ground. A little grunt escaped his throat, the sound of a man who has suddenly lost all his wind.

"It's been a good night of fishing," he added, "but I'm looking forward to that warm bed." He was drunk enough so that some of his words were slurring.

"Come on," I said, helping him to his feet. He felt like a bundle of twigs in my arms. He tried to put his arm around my shoulder but the fish between us made it difficult.

This fishing trip will be our final one, I thought, frightened. He won't last another month. At that moment I felt the weight of important things I needed to say. But I said nothing because if I let my attention turn inward, even for a second, I would begin to tremble and the tears would not stay back. The wind blew from the north and I shivered as it touched my cheek. I was worried for Ernie and all the human discord swirling around me in a time and place I could not understand.

Ernie died a few weeks later. During his last days, he was heavily sedated and spoke little. On the night of his death I had a dream. In my dream he came back and was at the foot of my bed, smiling and telling me it was good, this darkness, this place he had gone.

He left before I could tell him the things I wanted to say. I wanted to thank him for being my father, for helping me over the unfamiliar ground between child and man. I wanted him to know that he could look back and say, without blinking, that he had done right by me, his son. More than anything, though, I wanted to tell him how much I loved him.

I'll never forget the many wonderful things Ernie taught me. He thought he was only taking me fishing, but he filled me with enough memories to last a lifetime.

I'm still here, Dad. I'm still remembering…